Enemy Boss

Iona Rose

Some Books

Author's Note

Hey there!

Thank you for choosing my book. I sure hope that you love it. I'd hate to part ways once you're done though. So how about we stay in touch?

My newsletter is a great way to discover more about me and my books. Where you'll find frequent exclusive give-aways, sneak previews of new releases and be first to see new cover reveals.

And as a HUGE thank you for joining, you'll receive a FREE book on me!

With love,

Iona

Get Your FREE Book Here:
https://dl.bookfunnel.com/v9yit8b3f7

Enemy Boss

Copyright © 2024 Iona Rose

Publisher: Some Books

Chapter 1

Max

The club is heaving, and I can feel the pounding of the bass echoing through my body. The air is hot and humid. and I gulp down the last bit of water in my bottle and put the bottle down on the narrow counter running along the wall.

I am not getting any cooler so I decide to go outside for a bit of air. I turn to tell Harriet, my best friend, that I am stepping outside for a moment and that I might actually call it a night, but she's joined at the mouth with a guy she's met earlier. I shake my head with a smile and decide to leave her to it. I'm sure between her and the other girls who are off somewhere in the club, they will be able to work out that I've gone home.

I start making my way towards the exit.

The club is jam packed and I have to squeeze between writhing, dancing bodies, and by the time I get to the exit, I'm a whole lot more hot and bothered than I was on the dance floor. I make a promise to myself there and then that I won't come to a club if I'm stone cold sober ever again. The oppressive heat, the strangers being forced to stand too close to each other, and the incessant thump of the music are enjoyable when I'm drunk, but sober, they are awful. I wonder how any of the staff can stand to be there. I suppose it's slightly less packed behind the bar.

It is a relief to step outside. I take a long, deep breath of the cold air. I stand there until I feel goose bumps scurrying up and down my exposed arms. Crossing them in front of my body, I rub my upper arms, trying to get some warmth into them. My dress is cute; a barely there black bandage dress, but it really isn't suitable for the cold. Just like my heels aren't suitable for the concrete steps leading down from the club's door.

I start making my way down the steps carefully. Holding on tightly to the metal railing despite how cold it is against my hand. I look down, concentrating on my feet. What sort of idiot designs a place where people wear heels and drink alcohol to have concrete steps to get in and out?

I'm about halfway to the bottom when I feel my ankle roll.

I grab for the railing with my spare hand as my knees bend and I fall towards the unforgiving jutting edges of the steps. I don't hit the those gray stairs though. Instead, warm, strong hands catch and hold me until I manage to regain my footing. I look up, ready to thank my savior, but the words are stolen from my mouth.

I just look at him, my words momentarily lost, drinking in the sight of him.

He has tanned skin which perfectly complements the deep brown of his eyes. His hair is cropped short and for a second, I imagine running my hand over the silky strands. I imagine my hand moving lower, running over his arms and chest, which I can see through his t-shirt are muscular.

One side of his mouth curls up in a mocking smile and I realize I have been staring. I feel my cheeks flush and immediately I feel awkward, which brings on a surge of unreasonable anger inside me. As though it's somehow this stranger's fault that I was staring at him like a lost puppy.

"Thank you," I say huffily, self-consciously pulling down the edges of my dress.

"You're welcome," he says, but he doesn't move. His voice is low and gravelly, and I feel a shiver of desire go through me at the sound of it. I ignore the feeling and continue to frown at him. He's still so close I can feel the heat coming off his body... and he still wearing that irritatingly knowing smile on his face.

"Well?" I demand. "Are you going to get out of my way?"

He casually glances over his shoulder at the rest of the steps.

"Do you think you can make it that far unassisted?" he asks, unperturbed by my shocking rudeness.

"I'm not drunk you know," I blurt out.

"I didn't say you were," he replies, looking even more amused.

God he's annoying. And hot. Annoyingly hot.

"You implied I can't walk down a flight of stairs on my own," I say.

"Ah but I wasn't basing that conclusion off how much you may or may not have had to drink. I was basing that off the fact you have already almost fallen once and you're not quite half way down the stairs yet."

I know he's just teasing me, and I can't really argue his point either because he's right. Drunk I might not be, but my ankle is throbbing slightly, and my heels are too high. I have a feeling I will turn the ankle again before I reach the bottom of the stairs. Even so I can't give him the satisfaction of being right.

"Thank you again for catching me, but I assure you I am perfectly capable of getting down the rest of the stairs," I say firmly.

The smirk on the man's mouth becomes more of a grin as he waves his hand in the direction of the bottom of the stairs.

"Be my guest," he says.

He steps back enough to allow me space to move past him, but he makes no effort to carry on up the stairs towards the club. He watches me and I turn back to look him.

"Well?" he says.

"Go on then," I mutter grumpily.

"You go on. Looks like you're the one with something to prove."

I can hardly admit that I don't think I can make it the rest of the way down without hurting myself after I have been so adamant that I am just fine. I take a steadying breath and move down a step. So far, so good. I move down another one, but as soon as my already weak ankle hits the ground, pain flares up and my ankle rolls again. I don't even have time to grab for the railing with my spare hand this time before the sexy stranger's big warm hands are on me.

He stops me from falling, but instead of letting go of me, he lifts me into the air and throws me over his shoulder in a rather undignified fireman's lift.

"Put me down this instant," I demand, one hand thumping against his back and the other desperately trying to make sure I am not flashing my ass to the people coming and going from the club, some of whom are laughing at my predicament.

"Your ass is fine," the man says. "In more ways than one."

I ignore his strange compliment just like he ignores my command for him to put me down. I keep thumping weakly on his back as he moves down the steps, but the truth is, it's at best a token protest. It's good to get to the bottom of the stairs without further hurting my ankle and yes, I admit it, it feels good to be on his man's shoulder, his arm around my legs. I like the strength of him, the way I feel safe propped high up here. I like the warm, masculine smell of him too. Very nice. Very, very nice.

We reach the bottom of the stairs, and he slaps one hand against my ass. I yelp in indignation rather than any pain as he sets me back on my feet.

"Now we're acquainted, I should introduce myself. I'm Cullen," he says.

"Max," I reply. "Do you always spank people within seconds of meeting them?"

"Only if they've been naughty," Cullen says, laughter twinkling in his eyes.

I swallow hard, his words leaving me speechless and despite myself, I'm wet and turned on. He probably sees my discomfort, but he has no idea how much I liked his words.

"I'm joking Max, relax," he says.

I feel a bit silly, and I smile, forcing myself to stop showing myself up. He's not flirting with me. He's just trying to lighten the moment. "I much prefer my girls to be naughty. I would never punish them for that."

Ok, maybe he is flirting with me.

"Well, I hate to disappoint you, but I'm most definitely a good girl," I say.

"Obviously," he says. "Because every good girl can be found falling out of a club at two am."

"Ok, I agree that wasn't my finest moment," I say, smiling. "But I really am sober. That's what makes it worse. If I was drunk, I probably wouldn't have fallen."

Cullen chuckles. "Or if you did, you wouldn't have cared."

"Exactly," I agree.

"You're leaving early. Is it bad in there?" he asks, jerking his head in the direction of the club.

"It's bouncing, but when you're sober, it's awful. Too full, too loud, and way too sticky."

"With a recommendation like that, I think I'll give it a miss. Come on."

He starts to walk but I don't follow him. I'm not his little toy to boss around. He looks back over his shoulder at me.

"What?" he asks. "Are you waiting for me to carry you again?"

He starts back towards me, and I shake my head, knowing that he will actually pick me up.

"No," I say. I lift one of my feet up and slip my shoe off. "Just getting rid of these."

I slip the other one off and walk towards him, my shoes dangling from one hand. He's walking in the direction of the taxi rank anyway so I may as well walk with him as walk alone. I tell myself that's the only reason I am following him, the only reason I am still talking to him.

We are about half way to the taxi rank, crossing the parking lot for the club and the restaurants and bars that line the street alongside it, when he puts his hand in his pocket and pulls out a car key. He presses the fob and a sleek Audi beeps into life. Cullen veers away from me and heads for the car.

"See you around," I say.

He frowns at me.

"Playing games Max?" he asks.

I shake my head. "No game. I'm fine. I'll get a cab."

"Yeah?"

I know I should put my foot down here and go and get a cab, but there's something about Cullen, something intriguing. His very presence pulls me in and makes me want to spend more time with him. I will be honest – what most people would call charm is coming off to me as arrogance, like he thinks he only has to say the word and I will follow his instructions. But he's not wrong. There is something in his tone that is both commanding and also soft, like he isn't giving me an order, but explaining a foregone conclusion.

"Yeah," I confirm. "I just want to get a cab, go home, and wash my feet."

"Are you worried I'll kill us both? I've come straight from the office and Scout's honor, not a drop of alcohol has passed these lips."

I looked at his lips. If he's an axe murderer, he is one hell of a gorgeous one. I hadn't even thought of his sobriety and that is bad. I should have. But I do feel reassured knowing he hasn't had a drink. And not because of his driving skills. But because it means this flirting thing isn't one sided between sober me and drunk him. He's as sober as I am and he's not holding back.

"It's not that," I say slowly. "My mother told me not to get in cars with strangers."

"Really?" Cullen asks with another of those damned sexy grins. "And do you always do what your mom tells you to do?"

I do what I've *never* done before. I shake my head and start walking towards his car.

"Nope," I say as I open the passenger side door and get into the car.

Cullen gets into the driver's seat and pulls on his seat-belt. I like that. It tells me that despite his arrogance, there was still a part of him that wasn't sure if I was going to follow his orders or not. As Cullen watches me, I put my heels back on. He's still looking at me when I finish.

"What?" I ask, looking back at him.

"Put your seatbelt on," he says.

"Aww... are you worried about me?" I tease.

"I'm worried you might crack the windshield if you hit it," he says expressionlessly.

I can't help but laugh softly as I put my seat belt on. "Well, we can't have that can we."

He shakes his head, puts the car into gear and pulls off. He leaves the parking lot, turning right. He needed to turn left to get to my place and I tell him so. He grins at me, a grin so full of lust that I feel my whole body tighten. Between my legs an incessant throb begins.

"Isn't it time we stopped pretending you are going anywhere but back to my place?" he says.

The good natured flirting has been replaced with an intense sexual air that leaves me feeling breathless and I just nod because to even try to resist him at this point would be futile and I don't trust my voice to come out sounding even.

"Good," he says.

He puts his hand on my knee, and I feel tingles spread up my leg and to my pussy. It takes everything I have not to squirm on the seat. If he can make me feel like that with his hand on my knee, what is he going to be able to do with his hand further up? With his mouth? With his cock in me? A rush of warm lust floods me and I glance at Cullen. His eyes are on the road, but that smirk is completely gone, and I think maybe he felt it too where his hand touches me.

When he has to take his hand away to switch gears, I miss his touch. When he has changed them, but his hand goes back to the steering wheel, it is hard to hide my disappointment, although I think I manage it, because he would be grinning like a Cheshire cat if he knew how much taking away his touch had affected me.

We don't speak much for the rest of the drive, but I keep glancing at him out of the corner of my eye, and several times, I catch him looking at me too. The air is charged with lust, and in my fevered brain I feel as if I can almost see sparks flying around in the air. I've never felt anything like this before, and certainly not this quickly.

If someone had told me I was going to meet a guy and go home with him within five minutes of that meeting, I would have told them they were crazy. Yet here I am. And the strangest part is that it doesn't feel wrong and although I am a bit nervous, I'm more nervous that I might say or do something stupid rather than being nervous because I am going home with a stranger.

Finally, he turns the car off the road and down a driveway. He stops outside of a garage, but he makes no effort to open the garage door. He cuts the engine and I realize he's leaving the car there. I look up at the house as we get out of his car. It's a massive house, the front painted white, with a wrap-around porch. The garden is nicely kept as is the front of the house.

We get to the front door and he unlocks it and steps in, gesturing for me to follow him inside. I do and he closes the door and locks it. Then he smiles at me. A slow, sexy smile that turns my insides to jelly.

"Do you want to pretend you're here for the tour, or do you want to go upstairs and have the best orgasm you've ever had?"

He's very arrogant, very self assured. They aren't traits I generally like in a man, but Cullen pulls them off. I look up at his face, my mouth suddenly dry, my chest heaving.

"The ... the second one," I stutter.

"Wise choice," he says.

Chapter 2

Max

He takes my hand in his and leads me up the stairs. I follow behind him willingly enough, taking in the cream walls, the wooden floors. At the top of the stairs, there is a decent sized landing and leading off it there are four doors. Cullen leads me towards the first one on the left. He opens the door and steps inside. I follow and he kicks the door closed behind us. I flinch at the sound suddenly aware of just how quiet it is in here.

Cullen's room is also painted cream, and his furnishings are all made from dark oak, a perfect contrast. The wooden floor is broken up by several white rugs and the large bed is made up with white bedding and a black runner midway down it.

The interior designer in me smiles approvingly. The space is a perfect representation of what I have seen from Cullen so far – strong, masculine, commanding. I don't have long to appreciate the décor before Cullen is leading me towards the bed. He stops just before we reach it and turns me to face him. I think he is going to kiss me now and my lips tingle in anticipation, but instead, he leans down and takes a hold of my purse. He pulls it gently from my hand and throws it to one side. For a second, I can't help but think of my cell phone in there, but Cullen's fingers are grazing my thighs, and I can't think of anything but his touch. His fingers move to the bottom of my dress. He peels it over my head and leaves me standing before him in my heels and a lacy matching set of black underwear.

I reach out for him, but he shakes his head and takes a half step back. Unsure of myself suddenly, I stop and let my hands fall back down to my sides. Cullen smiles and closes the gap between us again. He takes my shoulders in his hands and spins me around so that my back is to him. He opens my bra, and it falls off my arms and to the ground. I kick it away, not wanting to trip over it. Cullen pulls me backwards until my back is pressed up snugly against his chest. He leans in and runs his tongue slowly down my neck and along my collar bone, making me moan with longing.

His hands start on my stomach but as he kisses back along my shoulder, they move up my body until he is kneading my breasts in time with his kisses. My nipples pop up and rub against Cullen's palms, sending delicious tingles through me.

Cullen kisses his way back up my neck and I turn my head so that my lips reach his. As we kiss hungrily, Cullen moves his hands away from my breasts. For a moment, I miss his touch, but then I feel his hand slipping into my panties and I no longer care about my breasts; it's all about my pussy.

Cullen moans into my mouth when he feels how wet I

am and as his fingers start to massage my clit, I press myself back against him, feeling his hard cock against my ass cheek.

It's my turn to moan as Cullen ups the pace of his fingers on my clit, sending me into overdrive as my orgasm hurtles towards me. I move my hips, pressing myself desperately against Cullen's fingers as the need to come builds up inside of me. As Cullen keeps working on me, he pulls his mouth from mine and puts his lips close enough to my ear that when he talks, I feel his lips moving.

"Don't come yet," he whispers, and the sound of his voice, and the commanding tone are almost enough to make me do the exact opposite and go falling into oblivion, but I hold myself back, wanting to see what Cullen is going to do to me next.

He moves his spare hand around my back, keeping me on the brink of climaxing with the other one. He pushes my panties down and they fall to the ground. I step out of them and kick them away. Cullen's hand moves up my spine and when it is between my shoulder blades, he pushes me forward, bending me at the waist a bit.

His hand trails back down my spine and over my ass cheeks. He presses it between my legs, and I side step with one foot, opening myself up to him, desperate for his touch to come to the place where I crave it most. He doesn't disappoint me. He pushes two fingers inside of me and pumps them in and out of me, keeping pace with the hand that teases my clit.

The double sensation is too much for me to bear and although I try to hold myself back, I can no longer remember why I want to do that, and I let myself go. My orgasm engulfs me and consumes me, and I feel like I'm floating. I can feel my pussy clenching around Cullen's still pumping fingers and my clit pulses against his other hand. Juices drip from me, running down my legs, and coating my inner thighs. My whole body feels alive.

Cullen moves his hand from my clit and pulls his fingers out of me, but my orgasm doesn't end there. The after tremors still buzz through me, delicious little trails of fire that catch me unaware and take my breath. I start to straighten up, but Cullen's hand is on my back keeping me down. Before I know what's happening, he spanks my ass hard enough to sting. I open my mouth to ask him what the fuck he thinks he's doing, but instead, a moan escapes out of me as the stinging pain turns into pleasure and sends a shudder through my body.

"You broke the rules Max," Cullen says. "I told you not to orgasm yet and what did you do?"

I don't answer him. Partly because I don't know what to say and partly because my face is pressed into his duvet, and I don't think he would hear me anyway. I gasp in shock and pleasure as he runs his fingers from my clit to my pussy and back again.

"And look how wet you are," Cullen says. "You still want more don't you?"

I nod my head.

"Answer me," Cullen demands, taking his hand off my back and allowing me to lift my head up.

"Yes," I say.

"Louder," he demands.

"Yes," I say again, practically screaming it this time.

Chapter 3
Max

I hear the rustling sound of clothing being shed behind me and then a different sort of rustling – the sound of a condom packet opening. I know Cullen is about to penetrate me, but that doesn't take away the delight I feel when the moment happens. Cullen's hands are on my hips, holding me still as he slams into me. There is nothing gentle about his penetration of me. He fills me in one long, hard stroke and I open my legs further, trying to make room to accommodate his huge cock. I can feel myself stretching as Cullen pulls back almost all of the way out of me and then he slams back into me once more.

The force of his thrusts takes my breath away, but they wake something up inside of me, something primal and full of allure. I'm not exactly a virgin, but I have never ever felt anything like this before. I find myself moving with him, pushing myself back against him as he pushes into me, wanting to feel myself filling up with him, wanting every inch of him inside of me.

I cry out his name as I move towards another orgasm,

but I have learned my lesson and I hold myself back, stopping myself from coming. It is both delicious and agonizing and I don't know how long I can do it for, but I am going to try and hold on until Cullen tells me it's ok to come. Strangely, I find that I want to please him, and more than that, I want to know just how intense my orgasm will feel if I can hold it back for a while longer.

I know I'm not the only one who is close to coming. I can hear Cullen's breathing growing ragged as he pumps into me, and his thrusts get harder and faster. He says my name in a voice filled with lust and it almost pushes me over the edge, but I force myself to focus on something other than how good his voice sounds and how amazing he feels between my legs.

I concentrate on how my breasts move beneath me, the duvet tickling my nipples with each thrust as I brace myself on my hands. That doesn't help. It just teases me. I also can't think about how my clit is tingling, the promise of a second orgasm stimulating it. I can't think of the way Cullen's hands feel on my hips, how the way he holds me and moves me back and forth on his cock make me feel like he never wants to let me go. And I certainly can't concentrate on the scent of Cullen's aftershave mixed with the scent of our lust.

One of Cullen's hands moves from my hip and comes around the front of my body. He pushes his fingers between my lips and rubs them over my swollen clit. I grimace, fighting with everything I have not to come. He opens and closes his fingers on my clit in a scissor like movement and I whimper, the pleasure too much for me, the need to explode too great.

With his fingers still tormenting me in the best possible way, his other hand grabs a fist full of my hair and pulls, lifting my head up. Cullen bends down to meet it, his body pressing against my spine.

"Come for me," he whispers, and I let go with a relief that is so great I almost cry.

He straightens back up and releases my hair and I grind myself down onto his hand and back onto his cock and I explode, my pleasure surrounding me and taking over every part of me. My clit pulses and my pussy tightens up around Cullen's cock. My stomach swirls and my nipples tingle. My body goes rigid, my muscles tense up, and my spine arches, pushing my head and my ass up as my stomach pushes down.

I can't breathe, I can't think. My mouth hangs open in a silent scream as my nerves all tingle and pulse. Red dots explode in front of my eyes, dancing flames that match the fire within me. I feel my eyes rolling back in my head and the room disappears leaving my vision black with only the dancing red lights for company.

I feel like I'm out of my body, like Cullen's cock is the only thing keeping me from floating away on a cloud of pleasure that is so intense it's almost agony. But such sweet agony. An agony I would happily beg for.

Slowly, my orgasm begins to fade. My eyes roll back into place as the red spots slow down their swirling and then vanish altogether. I find that my arms have collapsed, the muscles gone to jelly, and I half lay on the bed, my cheek on the cool duvet. I think only Cullen's grip on my hips is keeping my legs from collapsing out from beneath me.

I gasp in a long, shuddering breath and it comes out with a whisper of Cullen's name. He slams into my one more time and holds me in place against him, his cock pressing against my cervix as he fills me all of the way and explodes inside of me. He growls my name, and a shiver goes through me at the sound of it. My clit pulses once more and it's so tender but already I want more of him.

He slips out of me when his own orgasm has faded and I lay in place on my front, barely caring that my ass is in the air. I watch as Cullen ties off the condom and drops it into a waste paper basket at the side of the bed.

At first glance, he looks unaffected by what we just did, but when I study him for a moment, I see the way his eyes sparkle and the way he moves differently, like his thighs ache from fucking me so hard. He runs a hand over his head.

"Fuck," he says.

Maybe he came as undone as I did after all because his voice is a little shaky and he looks at me in surprise and shakes his head.

"Fuck," he says again.

I force myself to stand up from the bed, but I don't think my legs will hold me for long, so I quickly turn around and flick back the duvet and sit down on the sheet. I kick my shoes off, and then I move back a little bit so that I'm not perched right on the edge of the bed and Cullen smiles down at me, his composure well and truly back in place.

"Don't get too comfortable there," he says.

"Why? Are you kicking me out?" I say with a raised eyebrow.

Cullen's only answer at first is a soft laugh and then he

moves towards me and pushes me onto my back, climbing onto the bed between my legs. He leans back and opens the drawer in his bedside cabinet. He pulls another condom out and a shiver of desire goes through me as he opens it.

"Nope. I just don't want you falling asleep before I'm finished with you," he says.

He puts the condom on, casting the wrapper aside, and he moves himself on top of me, taking his weight on his elbows. I can feel his cock pressing against my soaking wet slit and I can't believe he is hard again already. I'm in no way complaining, but the shock must show on my face because Cullen smiles his lazy smile and runs his lips lightly over mine.

"It seems you have quite the effect on me Max," he says and the sound of my name on his lips turns me on so much.

I can't stop myself. I feel like a starving animal that has been given food for the first time in weeks. I spread my legs wider and reach down and take hold of Cullen's cock. I move it until it's lined up with my pussy. Cullen seems to want this as much as I do because as soon as I have his cock in place at my opening, he is pulling my hand away and pushing himself inside of me.

We move together, our bodies in perfect sync with each other. My hands roam over Cullen's back and sides as he kisses me, first on the lips and then on my neck. His thrusts get harder and faster, his cock assaulting my g spot with every movement. I am on the verge of another orgasm, and I can see by Cullen's expression that he is close too.

"Come with me," Cullen commands, and then he pushes into me all of the way and stays there, his body going rigid on top of mine as he comes. His cock spasms against my g spot and my own orgasm grips me.

I dig my nails into Cullen's ass cheeks, pressing him further into me as I clench tightly around him and my body tingles with pleasure. I move my hands up Cullen's back and cling to him as another wave of pleasure washes over me.

My tightened muscles relax and a warm, sated feeling washes over me as my orgasm subsides. Cullen has his face pressed against my neck as the last of his orgasm goes through him. His body shudders and then he pulls out of me and deals with the condom. He lays down beside me and we lay in the dark, our chests heaving as we get our breaths back.

As Cullen's breathing evens out and becomes the long, deep breaths of sleep, I feel a pang of regret. I don't know what I was expecting but somehow, it wasn't this. I guess I thought we might cuddle up together and fall asleep in each other's arms. I should have known that was a stupid thought. It's not like Cullen and I are a couple. We aren't even dating. It was just a spur of the moment thing that happened. Of course we aren't going to get all cuddly. And if I had had any doubt in my mind as to whether this was a one-night thing or the start of something, I have my answer now, and that's ok. I won't lie – I am a bit gutted to think that I will most likely never have another orgasm like those I have had tonight again, but I came back here tonight with no expectations, and I will walk away tomorrow with my head held high.

Chapter 4
Max

I wake up to a murky light coming in through the window. I guess it's still early and I close my eyes and start to snuggle back down to grab another few hours of sleep when I remember where I am. My eyes fly open, and I glance over my shoulder. Cullen is asleep beside me, and I take a moment to appreciate how damned good looking he is, even in sleep. I could easily let myself drift away and get lost in my memories of last night, but I don't. I really don't want the awkward morning after the night before conversation we would be forced to have if I stay here until Cullen wakes up.

With that in mind, I get out of the bed slowly, trying not to jiggle the mattress. When I'm back to standing on solid ground, I glance back over my shoulder. Cullen hasn't moved and I say a silent thank you and then I go over to where my underwear and dress have been thrown. I step into the panties, wishing I could go commando rather than wear yesterday's panties again, but my dress is too short for me to dare to do that. I pull my panties up and then I put my bra back on and finally, I pull my dress back on. I turn around to get my shoes and purse and I sneak towards the bedroom door, carrying my shoes for now as well as my purse.

I reach the door and put my hand out to press down on the handle and open it. I am almost touching the handle when Cullen speaks from behind me.

"I see you're leaving without saying goodbye," he says.

Dammit. I cringe inside, but I turn towards Cullen and smile, hoping I can be brazen enough to pull off the lie that's formed in my mind.

"I didn't want to wake you up," I say.

"And yet here we are," Cullen says with a grin that makes my stomach flip.

"Yes," I agree.

The silence stretches out between us, and Cullen keeps watching me. I can feel his eyes on me and knowing how much of me he saw last night I feel myself starting to blush. Cullen's grin widens and I don't know what to say so I end up blurting out the truth.

"I don't know what to say or do at this point. I don't usually go home with strangers like this, and I have no idea what the etiquette is," I say.

"Yeah right," Cullen says.

"Excuse me?" I say, sure I have misheard him. Hoping that I have misheard him, because if not, he is practically calling me a slut.

"Oh, come on Max. I talk to you outside of a club for five minutes and you come home with me, and you expect me to believe you don't do this regularly? The way you tried to sneak out speaks volumes, as does how good the sex was," he says.

I'm staring at him, the horror that he thinks of me that way slowly being replaced by temper. Cullen laughs softly.

"There's no need to look like that. I'm not judging you for enjoying sex, I'm just saying you don't need to lie about it. Own your truth Max," Cullen says.

I can feel my temper rising. Cullen's condescending tone and the half smile still on his face makes me want to punch him. I settle instead for words.

"I am owning my truth. And my truth is I don't usually do this. If you don't believe me then whatever, but that doesn't make it any less true," I snap. "You have no right to sit there and judge me. Yes, I came home with a stranger, but you brought a stranger home. You're not better than me."

"I didn't say I was better than you. I am more than aware that I brought a stranger home, but I am not the one who is in denial," Cullen says. "I don't think that's anything to be ashamed of."

I want to throw something at him, the way he speaks with that cocky little half smile on his smug, gorgeous face. I can't believe I thought that smile was attractive last night. I want to knock it clean off his self-assured little face. I think about throwing one of my shoes at him, but I like these shoes and I really don't want to leave one behind and I think the effect would be lost if I threw a shoe at him and then came back to retrieve it.

"Fuck you Cullen," I say.

I open the door and storm out, slamming it behind me.

It's not quite closed before I hear Cullen laughing and saying, 'you already did that'.

Ugh, he's so damned annoying.

I march down the stairs and stop at the front door long enough to put my shoes on. I open the door and step outside and slam that door too for good measure. I have no idea where I am, and I set off walking in what I hope is the right direction for home. I will call for a cab once I am somewhere I recognize.

Chapter 5
Cullen

"What's wrong with you?" my brother, Liam, shouts over the music that pumps through the club.

"Nothing," I shout back. "Why?"

"You keep looking at the door and you seem on edge. Are you in some sort of trouble?" Liam shouts.

He thinks I'm expecting a fight. Should I tell him the truth? Nah. He'll think I'm crazy turning up at this club like this in the hopes that she'll be here. Yes, Max is a judgmental snob. Yes, she is kind of stuck up when she isn't caught up in the moment. But she's also the hottest girl I've ever seen with thick and shiny long brown hair and the freckles across her nose and cheek bones which she attempts to hide with makeup but doesn't quite manage to do so. Her eyes are a gorgeous hazel color and I can't forget how good she looked underneath me, her face screwed up as she came and came hard.

That night with Max was the best sex I have ever had, and I have had more than my fair share of it. She seemed to lose any inhibitions she had and just enjoy the moment and I loved that. It made me feel free to pleasure her and to take pleasure from her in a way I have never felt able to do before. Mind you, she soon proved she wasn't a free spirit in the way I thought she was the next morning.

That doesn't stop me from wanting to see her again. I mean I don't want to date her or anything like that. She is spoiled and would be so high maintenance. But I want another night like last week with her. I know it won't happen though.

When I woke up and caught Max trying to sneak out without waking me up, with no sign of a note anywhere, I knew she didn't want to see me again. I don't have her number or her surname. I don't use social media so I wouldn't know where to start looking for her on there. Which means I have tried the one thing I could try and that hasn't worked. I don't let myself think about the fact that I have a private investigator that would likely find her in less than a day even with nothing more to go off than a first name and a physical description.

No, the universe has spoken again. It spoke last week, having me turn up just in the nick of time to meet Max. And now it speaks again telling me I won't be seeing her again.

"Of course not," I reply.

Liam smiles.

"What?" I say, not liking where this is going at all.

Liam's smile widens and he laughs and claps me on the shoulder.

"It's a woman, isn't it? My little brother is in love," he says.

"It's not a woman," I say, and I know Liam isn't convinced because even to my ears my words sounded like a lie. I sigh and roll my eyes. "OK. It's a woman. But I'm not in love with her. I only met her once. I just thought she might be here tonight. But she obviously isn't so I'm ready to go whenever you are."

"Now," Liam says. "You know how much I hate this place."

I nod my agreement and Liam and I cross the dance floor and leave the club. As we walk down the concrete stairs, I can't help but think of Max and how she fell and if she hadn't have done that, we likely wouldn't have spoken let alone anything else. I keep my expression neutral, not wanting to give Liam any more ammunition against me. He of all people should understand enjoying the single life because he loves it himself.

We get to the bottom of the stairs and start across the parking lot, heading to Liam's car. We reach it and he unlocks it with a beep of his fob. He gets in and I approach the passenger side door. I take one last look at the club and my heart does a double beat. Max is there at the top of the stairs with some other women. We must have literally missed each other by a second or two.

I know the moment Max spots me. It feels like the world stops for a moment as her eyes lock on mine and we just look at each other across the parking lot. Maybe the universe wanted us to meet again after all. Should I go back? Can I stand the teasing from Liam?

I'm about to go back when the passenger door window rolls down.

"Come on Cullen," Liam says. "Let's go."

His voice breaks the spell and I look away from Max and open the door. Of course I'm not going to go back. Universe be damned. Max is hot and the sex is amazing, but as a person, she sucks. I am not going to go running back to the club for someone I don't even like all that much.

Chapter 6
Cullen

One Year Later

"So, what's this really about Mom?" I ask before taking a forkful of her amazing chicken pasta bake, my favorite meal from when I was a young child and still my favorite meal now. I put it into my mouth and move it from side to side with my tongue as it burns my mouth and then I chew it, making an "umm" sound as it cools slightly, and flavor hits me.

"What do you mean Cullen? Can't a mother invite her son over for lunch and make his favorite meal without there being an ulterior motive?" my mom says, the twinkle in her eye telling me that I'm right to be suspicious of her motives.

I smile and shake my head as I swallow my mouthful of chicken pasta bake.

"Of course they can," I say. "But don't think I didn't spot that banoffee pie on the side earlier. My favorite meal and my favorite desert. That has to be more than just a casual lunch."

"OK, you got me," my mom admits with a grin. "I did want to ask you a favor as it goes."

"Fire away," I say.

Whatever she wants, I'll give it to her if it's within my ability to do so. She has done everything for me and Liam, me even more so because I'm the youngest, and she deserves the world. My father died in an accident when I was four years old. If I'm truly honest, I don't really remember him, although I do have all of my mom's memories of the things, he and I did together in the short time we had each other. It sounds like he was a good, attentive husband and father and I know my mom still misses him to this day, twenty six years later.

Once he was gone, my mom didn't allow herself to wallow in grief and self-pity. She threw herself into being both mom and dad to Liam and me and making sure we never went without. At one point, she worked three jobs just to make sure we had a roof over our heads and food on the table.

I think it's fair to say I owe her everything, although she would disagree and say she only did what any mom would do.

"Do you remember Hayley who I worked with a few years ago?" my mom asks.

I nod my head.

"Vaguely," I say. "I remember you talking about her, but I think I only met her once or twice though."

"Right. Well, she's got this daughter, Lucy. A nice girl by all accounts. She's twenty five and ..." my mom is saying.

As much as I love her, and I would do anything for her – or almost anything – I have to stop this before it goes any further. There's a line between me doing my mom a favor and me embarrassing myself.

"Mom, stop," I say. She looks at me, the surprise clear to see on her face, but she does stop. "Don't look so shocked. You know how I feel about being set up with people. It's cringe worthy, and even more so when it's your mom that decides to play Cupid."

Her shocked look vanishes, and she laughs and shakes her head.

"No, you don't understand," she says. "I don't want you to date this girl."

I laugh with her.

"Ok, sorry," I say. "Just it sounded like that's where it was going."

"Yeah, I see that now, but no. Definitely not. I have learned my lesson with trying to get you boys to be anything but eligible bachelors with Liam," she says.

I smile to myself as I finish up the last mouthful of my pasta. I definitely got off lightly there. She tried for a few years when Liam was in his late twenties to fix him up with someone. She gave up eventually, but not before Liam was about ready to emigrate.

My mom sees my empty plate and stands up from the table.

"I'll get those," I say, also standing up, but she waves me back down.

"I am perfectly capable of taking a few plates to the kitchen Cullen Monroe," she jokingly chides me. "I'm only sixty-one. Don't start looking for the nursing home just yet."

"What? You mean I will have to cancel the visit I booked?" I say.

She swats at me with her empty hand and we both laugh. She takes the plates and cutlery through to the kitchen and I hear her bustling about. She returns with two more plates and two more forks. Each plate contains a big slice of the banoffee pie I spotted earlier and a scoop of vanilla ice cream.

"Thanks mom," I say as my mom puts the plates down and then sits back down. I take my first bite and moan in appreciation. "I swear this gets nicer every time. Heaven on a plate."

My mom beams and I love how happy she looks in that moment. The moment passes and we work on our deserts.

"So, what were you telling me about this girl? Lucy, is it?" I say.

"Yes, Lucy. She's just got out of a relationship. Her ex-boyfriend is a nasty piece of work. He beat her by all accounts and when she finally got up the courage to leave him, he began to stalk her," my mom says.

"It sounds like she needs the police," I say.

"She tried that. But because she didn't want to press charges, she just wanted him kept away from her, there wasn't much they could do. They advised her to get a restraining order, but like she said to Hayley, if the man is willing to beat her, and risk those consequences if she went to the police, he's not likely to let the consequences of breaking a restraining order stop him from going after her," my mom explains.

It makes sense. The sort of dead beat guy who would hurt a woman like that probably isn't bright enough to understand what a restraining order even entails. I nod for my mom to go on. While Lucy's story is sad, and I admit I am curious to know where it's going, I still don't really know what it has to do with me.

"In the end, she did the only thing she felt like she could do. She got a new cellphone number, blocked him on all of her social media sites, left her job and moved to a new house," my mom says.

"Wow. That's a bit drastic isn't it," I say.

My mom shrugs.

"Maybe, but it seems to have worked. She's been in her new apartment for a week or two now and he hasn't bothered her since then," she says.

"Oh well, that's something," I say. "It's a shame because she's had to be the one to uproot her life even though he's the one in the wrong. And she's always going to have to be extra careful about who she trusts with her cellphone number, her address and stuff like that. Because I bet you that she has so called friends who will sell her out. Most people do."

"Yes," my mom says, nodding her head in agreement. "Hayley said the only people who have her new details are herself and Harriet, Lucy's best friend."

I think as I finish up my desert. It sounds like Lucy has hit a rough patch and maybe needs some money, but I know my mom would never ask me for money, especially not for someone I don't even know. She hates that I bought her a house when my company hit the big time. She wouldn't come to me for money for herself or anyone else. So, what does that leave? Maybe the girl is so scared she wants a body guard or something and my mom wants me to find one for her.

"The problem Lucy has now is that her savings are almost gone and she's on the verge of having nothing to live on. Hayley will help her out with her rent and the like where she can, but she's not exactly rolling in money herself," my mom says.

Maybe she is going to ask for money. If she does, she can have it. As much as she needs. Lucy and Hayley must be important to her for her to come to me with this and that means they are important to me too.

"She needs a job and she's struggling to find anything. That's where you come in," my mom says. "Can you give this woman a job at your firm?"

My heart sinks. It's the one thing I can't do. My company, ITSafe, is a professional company that helps other companies with cyber protection and it's not something where I can just employ anyone. They have to have an idea of what they are doing.

"I'm sorry Mom," I say. "I can't just hand jobs out like that. My clients rely on the company to deliver a certain level of service and if I have people around me that don't know their jobs properly, the whole thing can fall apart in mere minutes. What about if I cut her a check that will see her through the next three or four months so she's in a more comfortable place to find a job."

"No, she wouldn't accept charity," my mom says. "She doesn't want to be a freeloader. She just wants a chance. And I thought you said your secretary was going off on maternity leave. soon"

"She is," I say.

"And you haven't found a replacement for her yet, right?" my mom goes on.

"No," I say, not wanting to get her hopes up but not wanting to lie to her either. "But I need to get someone from the employment agency I use because I need someone who can hit the ground running. The crossover period for training is too short to put a pity hire there."

"No, I get that. And she wouldn't be a pity hire. She has plenty of administration experience. She was the PA to the CEO of the company in her last job," my mom says.

"Really?" I ask.

"Scout's honor," my mom says.

I ignore the fact my mom wasn't even a girl guide, let alone a scout, and I feel myself nodding my head, despite my reservations.

"Ok," I say. "Tell her to come to the office and find me at nine thirty on Monday morning. Tell her the post is temporary, a year's contract, to cover maternity leave with a chance of a permanent contract if she does well. Please also make it known that you might have gotten her through the door, but she needs to be able to do the job to stay. I know this family means a lot to you Mom, but I won't have her making a mess at my company."

Chapter 7
Cullen

"Yes," I say, lifting the receiver of my desk phone when I see it's an internal call and I know it's my secretary, Lisa.

"Hi Cullen," she says. "I have a Lucy Granger here. She says she has a nine thirty appointment with you, but I can't see anything on the calendar."

I can hear the mild chiding in her tone. She knows fine well Lucy is telling the truth about the appointment and that I have forgotten to update the calendar again, something she is forever having a go at me about. Strangely, getting told off by my secretary is one of the major things I will miss when Lisa is on her maternity leave. It's funny but being CEO of the company makes a lot of employees a bit nervous around me, and even the higher ups won't openly scold me. Lisa has no such issues.

"Send her in please," I say. "And can you add a nine thirty appointment to the calendar for me for today please."

Lisa laughs softly and I smile, picturing her shaking her head in amusement. As she hangs up the phone, I hear her telling Lucy to come through to my office and when there is a gentle tap on the door, I call for her to come in.

I don't know what I'm expecting Lucy to look like. I haven't really thought about it. What I'm not expecting to see is Max, a woman I slept with like a year or so ago. I am massively confused, especially when she comes closer to me extending her hand and announcing herself as Lucy Granger.

I stand up and shake her hand, sure I must be mistaken about her identity, but I know I'm not. I'm not in the habit of forgetting women I have had sex with, especially not when it was the sort of sex I had with Max. How could I forget that rose bud mouth, the hazel eyes and the cute smattering of freckles across her nose. And how could I forget the contours of her body, the places my tongue roamed over her skin, and the places that seemed made especially for my hands to fit on them.

"Cullen Monroe," I say, hoping my utter confusion isn't written all over my face. "Take a seat."

I don't know why Max has given a fake name or got my mom involved in whatever the hell this is. If she wanted to see me that badly, she could have just come up from the street and asked to see me. But I do know this – whatever game she's playing, it ends right here.

At first, I think she is either unaware of who I am or that she is unaffected by my presence, but then, as she sits down, I notice the flush of red on her neck and after a few seconds, she starts to fidget, crossing and uncrossing her legs and rubbing her hands together. I decide to just ask her what the hell is going on here. I don't have time to play games with her.

"Why did you lie about your name Max?" I ask.

The pink flush darkens and becomes red, and she scratches at her neck with her nails, and then she tugs slightly at the collar of her white blouse.

"I didn't," she says. "My real name is Lucy. Max is just a nickname."

That makes sense and it also explains why I couldn't find her on social media when I decided to try and look her up just out of curiosity months ago. I assumed at the time she had found me first and blocked me, but I guess I was searching for the wrong name. I am tempted to ask her why she has Max as a nickname, but it doesn't feel professional to ask and she isn't offering up the information, so I move on.

"And I suppose it's just coincidence that my mom is good friends with your mom then?" I say, raising an eyebrow.

"Yes," she says. "I had no idea that it would be you I was seeing today. I was just told to ask for the CEO – I didn't even know your name. Had I have known, I probably wouldn't have come, but the fact is, I need a job so if you're willing to give me a chance ..."

She trails off, leaving the rest unsaid. Having her here is the last thing I want. The attraction between us is still obvious, but so is the dislike. I don't want someone so uptight working for me, and I certainly don't want a secretary who dislikes me as intensely as Max does. But I do need a secretary and I haven't bothered contacting the agency since my mom gave me this solution, and I can't exactly let her go without my mom asking why and me having to admit to her that it was because I have slept with her, and it made things uncomfortable would be too much.

I find myself nodding my head.

"I'll give you a chance," I say. "But like I told my mom, your connection to her got you in the door. It won't keep you here. You have to be able to do the job to my standards to remain here."

"That won't be a problem," she says. "I have no issues keeping my personal and professional life separate."

"Good," I say. "You've done this kind of job before?"

I know she has, but I want to hear more about it. Max nods her head and tells me about her last role. If anything, it sounds more involved than what she will be doing here, and I am confident she will do just fine.

"Lisa goes on her leave next Friday," I tell her. "That gives her two weeks to show you how our systems work and what not. Will you be ready to hit the ground running?"

She nods her head and I lift up my desk phone receiver and call through to Lisa.

"Can you come into my office for a moment?" I say.

"Sure," Lisa replies.

She ends the call and a second later, she is tapping on my office door. I call for her to come in and she does, smiling questioningly at me.

"Do you need something?" she says.

"Lisa, meet Lucy, Lucy, this is Lisa," I say. The two women smile at each other, and I turn my attention back to Lisa. "Lucy will be filling in for you while you are on maternity leave. She has experience of this kind of role so you will only really need to train her on company specific software and our routine, that kind of thing."

"Ok," Lisa says. She smiles at Lucy again. "Let's get you set up on the system first and then we'll go from there."

Lucy stands up, ready to follow Lisa out of my office.

"If either of you need anything, let me know," I say. "Oh, and Lucy? The most important thing you need to know is coffee, cream no sugar."

I stop myself from smiling as I see Max bristle. She is going to absolutely hate having to bring me coffee and run my errands for me and what not, but unfortunately for her, it's a part of her job, and if it gives me a little bit of pleasure to ask her to do those things, well that just makes it a little bit more interesting doesn't it.

When the two women have left my office and the door has been pulled closed behind them, I wait a moment to give them a chance to get to Lisa's desk in case one of them comes back for something. When I'm sure they have gone, I turn to my computer and reluctantly sign into my hardly used Facebook account. I type the name Lucy Granger into the search bar and hundreds of results pop up. Only half a dozen or so have mutual friends and I spot Max in the profile picture of one of them. I click into it and begin to scroll.

Max's profile isn't private, and I can see all of her posts and pictures. She doesn't seem to post anything too private or controversial, hence the lack of privacy on the profile I suppose but she has posted some funny memes that I can't help smiling at, and even more so, I can't help smiling at her photos. There are photos of her with her friends on nights out and holidays, and there are selfies where she's pouting and others where she's laughing, presumably at herself for doing the pout pose.

I spot her standing on the beach in a skimpy orange bikini, her hair blowing out behind her and the sea in the background and my heart skips a beat. God this woman is absolutely gorgeous, and the irony of the situation is not lost on me. I am finally feeling ready to find a partner and settle down and this beautiful creature comes into my life for the second time, but as gorgeous as she is, I really fucking dislike her.

Chapter 8
Max

I'm still reeling as I sit down beside Lisa at her desk and watch as she logs in to her email account and types out a message to the IT department asking them to create logins for me to access all the company's programs. Once she's sent it, she starts showing me some of the programs she uses. I'm familiar with most of them, but a few are company specific, and I pay particular attention to those, although I have to admit that I'm finding it hard to concentrate on much of anything right now except for the fact that I have somehow managed to get myself employed by Cullen of all people. Honestly, it's something if someone else told me, I wouldn't believe it was a genuine coincidence. I thought shit like this only happened in movies but nope, here I am, starring in nothing but my disastrous life.

I couldn't believe it when I walked into his office and saw him sat there. I almost just turned around and walked back out again. Maybe I should have. But I seem to like torturing myself. And it seems that the universe is happy to comply with me on that one. I mean, come on. Out of every single person in the world, like seriously, what are the chances of me ending up working for the one guy I had a one night stand with who pretty much called me a slut afterwards?

If it wasn't for the fact that I am a week or two away from being absolutely broke and not being able to even make my rent, I would have turned around and walked out right there and then. But of course, the universe hates me so that wasn't an option. And to make things even worse, of course I still fancy the ass off of Cullen. I know he's not a nice person and he appears charming until after he gets what he wants and then he shows his true nature, but that doesn't mean he isn't hot to look at. It's just one more level of ridiculous in my life. The one guy I really fancy is a total douchebag and I know it, and yet I am still sitting here remembering how good his cock felt inside of me.

Walking into his office brought back a flood of memories and for a second, I felt like I was right back there on that night, like I wanted to walk around the desk, straddle Cullen on his chair and have him fuck me into oblivion. As nice as that does sound, there's no way I am going to let myself go there with him again. I don't care how good looking he is, or how good his body looks in his suit. I don't care that he made me orgasm in a way I didn't even think was possible. I don't care that he made my body sing in a way I haven't felt before or since being with him. I am not going there again. Never ever.

"Lucy? Are you ok?" Lisa asks from beside me.

I nod my head. I realize I wasn't really listening to her, that I had drifted off into a world of my own, but the program she is talking about is one I've used a lot and I know it inside and out, so I don't think I'll have missed anything important. She's looking at me strangely though and I feel like I need to say something.

"I'm fine why?" I say.

Lisa shakes her head.

"I don't know. You went all quiet and then your face and neck started getting red," Lisa says.

Great. Even my own body is working against me today. Thanks for that universe. Thanks a lot.

"I'm just a bit hot," I lie.

Well actually, it's not a lie. I am just not going to even hint on to the fact that I am

feeling a bit too hot because I am thinking about how Cullen's cock felt when it was

filling me up, and that it is nothing at all to do with the temperature in the room

Well actually, it's not a lie. I am just not going to even hint on to the fact that I am

feeling a bit too hot because I am thinking about how Cullen's cock felt when it was

filling me up, and that it is nothing at all to do with the temperature in the room

Well actually, it's not a lie. I'm just not going to even hint on to the fact that I am feeling a bit too hot because I'm thinking about how Cullen's cock felt when it was filling me up, and that it is nothing at all to do with the temperature in the room.

Well actually, it's not a lie. I am just not going to even hint on to the fact that I am

feeling a bit too hot because I am thinking about how Cullen's cock felt when it was filling me up, and that it is nothing at all to do with the temperature in the room

"Do you need to go outside and get some air or some-thing?" Lisa asks, still peering at me with concern etched on her face.

I shake my head and smile, forcing my attention back onto her and her screen and away from my wild imagina-tion. I feel kind of guilty that she looks so concerned. God what would she think if she knew the truth.

"No, honestly, I'm ok," I say.

Lisa looks at me for a second longer. I don't know if I was particularly convincing in my words or if the redness from my skin has started to fade back to normal, but either way, Lisa turns away from me and faces her screen again, continuing on with her tutorial. We go through several programs I know well and a few I don't, but they all seem user friendly enough, and I'm sure I will be fine with finding my way around them on my own once I have to. She shows me the filing system, both electronic and paper, and she shows me all around the building. By the end of the day, I'm tired, but satisfied. I feel like I have done well for my first day and I haven't seen Cullen since first thing this morning, which I consider as a win.

The next two weeks pass in a blur of learning and, by the end of week one I'm pretty much the one doing the job and Lisa is just observing me and only stepping in when I am obviously floundering or if something is going to go horribly wrong if she leaves me to roll with it. I've had to deal with Cullen a lot on the phone, and even a couple of times face to face, but it hasn't been so bad. He's been cool to me, but that's ok; he's my boss now and I don't expect anything else. I am also getting used to seeing him around and I find that I am no longer shocked at how handsome he is every time I see him now, although I do still find myself staring at him and unable to look away from time to time. What? He's good to look at. I can't help it.

Today is my first day of going solo and I'm determined to nail it. Lisa left me her cellphone number in case I need to ask her anything, but I really don't want to disturb her with work stuff now that she's no longer at work, so I'm going to try my best to muddle through if there's anything I don't really understand. As much as I tell myself I don't care what Cullen thinks of me, I care enough to not want him to think I can't do this job without Lisa to hold my hand.

My desk phone rings I'm opening up my programs on the computer and I reach for the receiver and bring it up to my face. I take a deep breath and smile so that I sound open and friendly.

"Good morning, thank you for calling ITSafe. You have reached Cullen Monroe's desk. How can I help you?" I say.

My greeting feels long and awkward when I say it. When Lisa said it, it always sounded natural, like it just flowed off her tongue. I make a mental note to change the greeting to something that feels closer to what I would say naturally while still maintaining the professional air that is required.

"I need to speak to Cullen please," a male voice says.

"Is he expecting your call?" I ask politely.

The caller snorts.

"I doubt it seeing as I didn't decide to call until a minute ago," he says.

"Ok," I say. "Let me see if he's available. Who should I say is calling?"

"Don't bother asking him, he wouldn't dare refuse my calls," the man says and laughs. "I'm his brother by the way."

"Oh, ok," I say, my smile becoming more real now I know it isn't an irate client calling to say I have made a terrible mistake already.

I remember Lisa telling me that Cullen is big on family and if his mom or brother calls to always put them through unless he is in with someone.

"I'll put you through now," I say, and I transfer the call and replace the receiver.

I turn my attention back to my computer and start going through everything Lisa taught me about my daily work in between taking calls and greeting any clients who visit. I soon get into the swing of my morning reports and message checking, and I smile to myself. This is, if anything, less intense than my last job. Back then, I would have fielded about twenty calls by now and that's on top of everything else I was expected to do. Here it seems that I can amble along at my own pace and that I won't be as bombarded with calls to disturb me either.

It's been about half an hour since Cullen's brother called when I hear Cullen's office door open. My desk is situated in the large, open space outside of his office and it's turned at an angle so that I can see people coming and going both from the corridor end and from Cullen's office. I can't see him until he actually steps out though.

I'm wondering if he has a new task for me or if he is going out somewhere when he steps into view. I swallow at the look of thunder on his face, his forehead creased, and his mouth set in a tight line of disapproval. I wouldn't want to be on the end of whatever telling off he is about to dole out. I look away quickly and turn my attention back to my computer, but Cullen doesn't stalk past. Instead, he comes over to my desk and when I look up at his glowering face, I realize I am in fact the one on the end of this telling off. Wonderful. So much for thinking I was nailing it. I am not even an hour in, and it seems that I've fucked up.

"What the hell was that?" Cullen demands.

I want to shrink back away from his temper, but I refuse to let him bully me and I force myself to hold his gaze.

"What was what?" I ask, genuinely baffled. I have no idea what I've done wrong.

"You put Liam through to me when …" he starts.

I thought he had finished speaking and so I start to explain to him, but then I realize, too late, that he hadn't actually finished at all and I have just interrupted him when he is already pissed off with me, but I think it'll be more awkward to stop now that he's gone quiet and let me cut in mid-sentence and so I go on, pushing the awkwardness to one side. At least for now.

"I was told that you will always take the calls from your mom and your brother, unless you are in with someone," I say.

"Or on a conference or video call," Cullen says.

I nod my head. I knew that; I just didn't feel the need to explain every tiny detail of what Lisa had told me.

"I was on a very important video call when you put Liam through to me," he says.

My heart sinks at his words and I shake my head.

"I ... I'm sorry. I didn't know," I say.

"It's your goddamned job to know," he says.

"I'm sorry," I say again.

He ignores my apology and goes on.

"Just because you personally didn't add something to my calendar, it doesn't mean it isn't happening. I suggest from now on that you make your first job of the day to refresh my calendar and see if there's anything new been added on there," he says.

"Ok," I say, trying to keep my voice steady. "I will do that from now on."

"See that you do," he snaps and then he stalks back to his office and slams the door so loudly that I cringe.

"Asshole," I mutter under my breath.

God how did I ever find him attractive?

Chapter 9
Max

I check the time. I have about half an hour before I have to go into a meeting with Cullen. Most of the rest of the office staff have left for the night and I am nervous. Not because I'm waiting alone, but because I am dreading the meeting. I shouldn't be, because it's to go over a report that I typed up for Cullen. I know everything on there is spot on and I have nothing to be afraid of, but Cullen has already snapped at me twice today already and I know that despite the report being perfect, he will probably find some reason to have a go at me. He probably won't like the font I used or the lay out of the information or something equally petty.

I go along to the breakroom with my cellphone. I'm going to grab a cup of coffee and call my best friend, Harriet. She will hopefully calm me down. God, I am so grateful to have her in my life. She's pretty much the only friend I have now. Since I moved away to get away from my ex-boyfriend, there's only Harriet who has my new address and cellphone number. It's not that I don't trust my other friends, but I know what my ex-boyfriend is like, and I know that he would find a way to charm the information out of them. That's partly my own fault because I didn't tell my friends how bad things had gotten between us. I always pretended that things were good, and that Ross was the perfect boyfriend. Even when we split up, I said it was just because we wanted different things and left it at that. I was ashamed to admit I was scared of him, that he was violent and controlling. Only Harriet knows the truth so only Harriet can be fully trusted not to leak anything to him.

We've been broken up for a few months now and I've been gone from where he can find me for almost six weeks, but I know Ross. When he wants something, he doesn't give up easily and he made it clear he didn't want us to break up and that he would find me and make me his again.

I push aside all thoughts of Ross. I hate it when my guard slips down like that, and I let the thoughts of him into my head. Now is an especially bad time for it to happen, because I'm nervous enough with this meeting looming ahead of me without having to start going back over old ground, old fears. I get myself a coffee and sit down with it. I blow on the surface as I scroll through my cellphone and find Harriet in my contacts. I hit call and bring the phone up to my face at the same time as I take a sip of the coffee. I wince. It's good, but it's still too hot. I put the cup back down to leave it to cool for a bit longer.

"Hey, you," Harriet says as she takes my call. "How's things?"

"Hi," I say. "Can you talk?"

"Well, it could be a problem between me having to focus so hard on the TV or on Rufus's snoring," she says with a laugh. I smile at the thought of Rufus's sweet little face. Rufus is Harriet's snuggle bug of a bull dog. "So, what I'm trying to say is yes, I am free to talk. What's up?"

"I have a meeting in," - I twist my wrist and look at my watch – "About twenty minutes with Cullen and I know he's going to find fault with my work. I just want someone to remind me I am not totally useless before I go in there."

"Oh, for lord's sake," Harriet says, and she huffs out a sigh. I picture her rolling her eyes at me. "I wish you two would just fuck already, get it out of your systems, and then you could stop thinking about him and he could stop doing the adult equivalent to pulling your pig tails to make sure that you notice him."

"It's not … that's not going to happen," I say.

"But it should," Harriet insists. "It really would help. And it's not like you don't want to. Don't lie to me Max, I know you do."

I sigh and sip my coffee which is now just on the right side of warm.

"He's hot, I'm not denying that. But he's awful as a person. He's moody and arrogant and all he seems to do is criticize me," I say.

"I'm not saying marry the guy," Harriet replies. "I'm saying fuck him. And if you don't want to hear the shit he talks, I don't know, sit on his face or something."

I burst out laughing at that and I instantly feel better. Harriet never fails to make me laugh about things that have been bothering me and it seems that Cullen making my life hell is no exception. I almost didn't tell her about Cullen and our history together, but now I'm glad I did.

"Seriously though, what do I do about him always

digging at me," I say.

"Is fucking him really out of the question?" she asks.

"Completely," I confirm.

Harriet thinks for a moment and then she speaks again.

"Ok, here's what you do," she says. "Forget you have shared history with him and think of him like any other boss. You wouldn't have gotten upset if your last boss had criticized your work, justified or not. Think of him only as your boss and let his words roll off of you. You know you're good at your job and despite moany pants having a go at you, he has kept you on, so he obviously knows it too and that's all that matters."

I smile and nod my head. It's good advice and she is right – with any other boss, I would just ignore the moaning and the digging. Some bosses just don't know how to manage people and that's ok, I can let that slide off me like Harriet said.

"I can do that," I say.

"I know you can," Harriet says. "And if all else fails, just imagine him naked."

"How will that help?" I say with a laugh.

"I have no idea but it's a thing, isn't it?" Harriet says.

"For interviews," I say.

"Interviews, meetings, whatever," Harriet says. "Now do you genuinely feel better, or do I have to come down there myself and kick this guy's ass?"

"No, you don't have to do that just yet," I say with another laugh. "And yes, I do genuinely feel better. I just have to remember that Cullen's opinion of me isn't important, and I will be fine."

"Exactly," Harriet says. "Or fuck him. Your call."

Chapter 10
Cullen

I sigh as I read over the next section of the report. Max watches me from the opposite side of my desk. I can't deny that I like her presence, like looking at her, but I miss Lisa's cool, quiet efficiency. It took me five minutes to get Max to stop the nervous babbling when she first appeared in my office. And then she looked confused when I snapped at her to be quiet so I could look over the damned report.

I know the majority of the information in it already – after all, I had been the one to provide it and have Max type it up in a cohesive form and then pull up several other reports to compare the information in them. It is that comparison that I am mostly interested in and also a large part of what this meeting is about, because the answers in the report comparisons will show me where we need to concentrate our marketing efforts next to get the best chance of getting new business.

I scan down the columns of figures, aware of Max's eyes on me as I read. I glance up and she looks away quickly, her face flushing with embarrassment at being caught watching me. I can't help but grin to myself. It's good to know that despite how much she annoys me at times, I can have that same effect on Max as she has on me. Even now, the sexual tension in the air hums around me and it's all I can do to concentrate on the report and not on her face.

I look back down at the report and my desire takes a back seat to frustration when I see the mistake Max has made on the next section of the report. I sigh loudly and look up at Max again. She is looking back at me, but this time, she has a questioning look on her face rather than a sheepish look.

"You fucked it up," I say. She opens her mouth to speak but I don't let her interrupt me and she closes her mouth again. I really could find better uses for that mouth than arguing with me. "How did you manage that?"

I turn the report towards her and point to the mistake. She shakes her head.

"No, I swear that's correct," she says. "I can go and get the old report I got the figures from and show you if you don't believe me."

"Not the old report figures," I say. "The latest ones."

"I just used what you gave me," she says.

Temper surges through me. It's bad enough that she is still making these little mistakes without lying about it as well. I can understand, perhaps, her making the odd mistake if it's on software specific to the company that she's never used before or something like that, but this was a simple case of copying information she had been given onto a new format.

"Are you trying to say that I fucked it up?" I say, raising an eyebrow along with my voice.

"I ... No. I'm just saying that I didn't," she replies.

I jump out of my seat and start to pace the floor to try and calm down a bit but it's hard as she peers at me, no sign of shame at her lies on her face.

"Two people had input on that section Max. Me and you. So, if you are so sure it wasn't you who made a mistake, then you must think it is me," I say.

She gives a half shrug of her shoulders, and the arrogance of the move sends me over the edge.

"Are you fucking with me woman?" I shout. "You don't get to make simple mistakes like this and then sit there and lie about them and then try to blame me for them. Do you understand?"

As I say the last part, I turn towards her and take a few steps closer to her. She doesn't say anything, she is just staring at me. I lift my hand to massage my temples where I can feel a headache starting. I haven't quite got my hand to my face when Max jumps up and runs for the door. She is out of my office before I can say anything, but not before I see the tears in her eyes.

I rub my temples in a circle as I curse under my breath. I went too far. I know I did. I just wanted her to admit the mistake and we could have moved on, but I know I shouldn't have yelled at her as much as I did. The poor woman probably thinks I'm going to fire her. I'm not – I just want her to be aware of these mistakes so she can be more careful and double check her work that's all. I won't always have the time to check everything behind her and if she's working on something for a meeting or a client, I need to be confident it's right the first time. If I have to double check everything she does, I might as well just do it myself in the first place. Surely, she can see that.

Still though, I know I was out of line the way I yelled at Max and with another sigh, I head for my office door so I can track her down and apologize to her. She's not at her desk. I quickly duck behind it and look into the foot well. Her purse is still down there where it always is, so I know she likely hasn't left the building and I figure the most likely place for her to have gone if not here is to the bathroom.

I head down the hallway to the ladies' bathroom and knock on the door. No answer.

"Max? Are you in there?" I say. Again, there is no answer, but I hear water running so I know she's in there. "Max, I'm coming in."

I give her a warning because it feels like the right thing to do before going into the ladies' bathroom, not that I think Max is going to be standing there naked or anything. I couldn't be that lucky.

I open the door and see Max standing before the sinks and the mirrors. Her face is red and blotchy although she has dried away the tears. I feel like the biggest bastard in the world for making Max cry. I would have felt awful for making anyone cry like this, but especially Max. She already dislikes me. Now she probably outright hates me.

"I'm sorry Max," I say.

She slowly turns her head from the mirror and looks at me.

"I appreciate that," she says. "But really, you don't need to apologize. I should be the one apologizing. I obviously made a mistake and then I got defensive about it. I'm sorry for that. And most importantly, I am sorry that I completely over-reacted."

I feel even worse now Max seems to feel like she has to apologize for having emotions, but I have to admit, now she's said it, I do think it was maybe a little bit of an over reaction. And despite Max's faults, I have never imagined her to be someone who is emotionally vindictive and would turn on the water works to get sympathy, so she must have been genuinely upset by what I said.

"I shouldn't have yelled at you like that. I was just frustrated that's all," I say, moving closer until I'm standing beside her. "I didn't mean to upset you."

She shakes her head and smiles at me, a sheepish smile that tells me that what she is about to say is embarrassing for her.

"You didn't upset me. Not really. I ... Just when you were yelling and then you came towards me like that. My ex would yell at me like that, and when he came towards me while mad like that, it was usually the start of him beating me. It just brought that back for a moment," she says. "You kind of raised your hand."

The bottom falls out of my world. I vaguely remember my mom saying something about her moving to get away from an abusive ex, but I didn't know he had hurt her to the point where she carried that fear with her around other people too. And now I have hurt her, scared her. I make a silent vow in that moment that if I ever meet her ex, I will make him pay for what he has done to her, for the expression now on her face, the one where she wonders if I will decide she deserved it.

"Oh Max, I am so sorry," I say. "I was raising my hand

to massage my temples because I have a headache. I would never, ever hurt you like that, I swear."

"I know," she says. "Like on a rational level, I know that. But sometimes, in the moment, rational thought goes out of my head and it's like I'm back there, just waiting for a fist to smash into my eye."

She looks so fragile in that moment and another tear runs down her face. I don't think about what I'm doing, I just act. I reach out and pull her into my arms. For a second, she stiffens, and I think I have made another horrible mistake, but then she relaxes and leans against me, her head on my chest. She puts her arms around me, and we just stand there like that for a moment as she gets herself back under control.

She pulls her head back but keeps her arms around me and so I keep holding her. She tilts her head back to look at me, her eyes scanning my face questioningly and then settling on my eyes. I can't look away from her and I feel the air in the room shift as lust fills me, mirroring the lust I can now see in Max's eyes.

I want so badly to kiss her, but I don't want to misread the situation or let her think I am taking advantage of her being upset. She doesn't seem to have those concerns because she reaches up with one hand and puts it on the back of my head and pulls my face down to hers.

Our lips touch and I feel fire run through mine, igniting my nerves and making me want this woman more than ever before. Her tongue pokes almost shyly into my mouth, but as I push mine against it, the shyness melts away and it is as though Max has been unleashed. Her tongue moves against mine, wrapping around it and then delving further into my mouth. She presses her body against me, her breasts against my chest.

She moves her hand away from the back of my head and brings it around the front of my body. Her other hand joins it, and she unbuckles my belt and then opens my trousers. She pushes them down and then my boxer shorts. Her movements are frenzied, and my body reacts to her touch. My cock is hard by the time she frees it from my boxer shorts, and she pulls her mouth from mine and looks at it in approval.

I pull her dress up around her hips and push her panties down. She has barely got one foot out of them when I lift her onto the counter between two of the sinks. I debate taking her back to my office rather than fucking her here in the bathroom, but it's just been cleaned, and I'm worried taking her back to my office will ruin the moment and kill the mood.

I nudge Max's legs open and step between them. She is already soaking wet. I can smell her lust on the air as I kiss her again and then I pull my mouth from hers and I start to plunge my cock into her pussy. Just in time, I stop myself and step back. Max looks at me, an expression of surprise on her face.

"What's wrong?" she says.

"I haven't got a fucking condom," I say.

She grins.

"I'm on birth control. Get back here," she says.

I don't need telling twice. I move back to my prime position between Max's legs, and I slam my cock into her eagerly waiting pussy. Filling her feels like coming home and I moan as I slam into her. She gasps and for a second, her thighs tighten around me and then she relaxes, and I begin to move inside of her.

She puts one hand on my shoulder. The other, she puts behind her ass and uses to brace herself, her palm flat on the counter top. She pushes against me, matching my thrusts with desperate little thrusts of her own. I put my hands on the bottom of her back where her skin is bare and push them beneath her dress, running my nails lightly over her skin. She gasps again and I can tell she's almost ready to climax as she begins to thrust faster, and her fingers dig into my shoulder.

I oblige her more than willingly, thrusting harder and faster into her and she moans my name as her orgasm hits her. She clenches around me, her pussy tightening on my cock and her thighs squeezing me. Her ass is half off the counter, my full length inside of her and she is leaning back on her palm, her head thrown back as her body shudders.

As she shudders, her pussy tightens again, and a rush of heat floods me. It's enough to push me over the edge myself and I pull halfway out of her and then I thrust back in and then my own orgasm washes over me, turning my body into a pleasure center, my muscles like jelly as I pull Max towards me and bury my face in her chest as I roar her name.

My orgasm grips me tightly and then it slowly starts to fade, and I gasp and pant. I can feel Max's chest rising and falling against my face and I know she's trying to get herself under control too. I stay where I am for a moment and then I straighten up and slip out of her.

I move back and Max hops down off the counter. She seems unruffled by our encounter, but the redness on her face and neck gives her away and the slightly glassy look in her eyes tells me she enjoyed that as much as I did. I mean how could she not? It was absolutely mind-blowing.

Max pulls her dress down and her panties up while I'm pulling my boxer shorts and trousers up. I'm still fastening my belt back up when Max grins at me.

"Apology accepted," she says in a breathy voice and then she turns and walks away from me, tossing her hair back over one shoulder.

She doesn't so much as look back as she leaves the bathroom and I'm left staring after her, my mouth agape. How can one woman be so irritating and yet so sexy all at once? How is it that I find myself wanting to not have to deal with Max again, and at the same time, already wishing I was balls deep in her once more?

I don't know the answers to those questions. I don't know how Max manages to both annoy me and turn me on to the point where I barely know who I am anymore. But I do know one thing – that can't be the last time I have her. Despite how much she winds me up, how much hard work she is, I know I want her again and again. I want her to be mine and mine alone.

I hadn't really realized how much I was falling for Max until I heard that her ex- boyfriend had hurt her to the point that it still haunts her now and the feeling it awakened inside of me, the longing to protect Max and keep her safe from the world, told me that I am in deep trouble here.

Chapter 11

Max

I still can't quite believe that I allowed what we did last night to happen again. I vowed never to go near Cullen again after the attitude he has shown me since I started working for him. I meant it whole heartedly at the time, but in the moment, it just felt right, and I was sick of depriving myself of what I wanted. I knew I would regret not letting it happen, and honestly, I am also sick of regrets. For once, I just threw all the rules out the window and did what I wanted to do in the moment and honestly, it felt good. Amazing even.

If only Cullen could always be the person he was last night when he came to find me in the ladies' room, but it's not that simple because Cullen is like two different people – there's the cold, snappy side of him which I don't care for at all, and then there's the sweet side of him, the side that leaves me feeling warm inside and like I could be with him. If it wasn't for the night we spent together before, I would have said the cold side was just his work persona, but he was rude to me that night too.

Was he though? The little voice inside of my head pops up at the worst times and questions my judgement. But does it have a point? I mean he did imply I slept around, but maybe it really had been a joke. Not a good one, certainly, but there might not have been any malice in it.

I don't even know anymore, but I tell myself that it doesn't matter either way because I've just done what Harriet told me to do – I have fucked Cullen and gotten him out of my system. Except that there's one problem with that and that is that he's still very much in there. At least he won't suspect as much. I am quite proud of the way I handled the moments after we had sex. I definitely got the upper hand and refused to let Cullen give me any more apologies or say it couldn't happen again or give me any of the platitudes I'm sure he had lined up for me. I thought my way was straight to the point and worked nicely to be honest.

So far today, I have encountered Cullen twice. The first time he barely grunted a greeting at me and the second time, he was equally as charming, snapping out an instruction like I was a dog he was in the middle of training, and it had pissed on his carpet, and walking away before I even had a chance to respond to him. It's good to know he's being mature about this.

It's almost eight o'clock now and I have finished my work for the day. I have a few things I need Cullen's signature on before they can go out. I could drop them in to him in the morning, but I decide instead to drop them in now, and hopefully he will deal with them first thing and then I can get on with them.

I gather the papers up and head for Cullen's office. He

will have left for the day by now, so I don't bother to knock on the door and when I open it and see him sitting behind his desk, I jump slightly. I open my mouth to apologize, but he gets in first.

"Come on in, make yourself at home," he says sarcastically.

I resist the urge to roll my eyes at him. I need this job and I can't afford to give him any excuses to get rid of me. Instead of rolling my eyes, I smile apologetically.

"I'm sorry," I say. "I thought you had left for the day. I'll just leave these here."

I indicate the papers and head towards Cullen's desk and put them in his in tray. He grunts at me again as I turn away from his desk and before I can stop myself, I whirl back around to face him.

"You can speak to me you know. You don't have to go all weird just because we had sex," I say.

I know I shouldn't have said it, but his silence is even worse than his snapping and to be honest, it's annoying me. So, we had sex. He should know from last time I don't expect anything more from him and he can speak to me without me thinking there's anything in it.

"You think that's why I've been quiet around you?" Cullen says, looking up and meeting my eye for the first time that day.

I nod my head, sure that my impatience is showing on my face.

"What else could it be? Nothing else has changed since yesterday," I point out.

"Under the circumstances, I can see why you would think that. I probably would have come to the same conclusion myself. But I can assure you what we did last night in that bathroom has nothing to do with this," he says.

I feel the heat flood my cheeks as he talks about last night, and my pussy responds to the memory, getting damp and sending a pulse of desire through my clit. I ignore the feeling, my eyes on Cullen, waiting for him to go on. When he doesn't, I sigh.

"So, what is it then?" I ask.

For a moment, Cullen doesn't say anything, but he does nod towards the chair opposite his and I sit down and wait for him to answer me. He must be planning on doing so, or at least saying something, or he wouldn't have gestured for me to sit down.

"I owe you an apology," he says. "About the report."

"You already apologized," I say, but he shakes his head.

"No. Last night I apologized for yelling at you over it. Tonight, I find that I must apologize for accusing you of messing it up in the first place. I have looked back over the report today and it was my mistake, not yours. I sent you the wrong figures. I've been off with you all day because I have been trying to work out a way to say I'm sorry," he explains.

"It's pretty simple really," I say, my feeling of joy that I had been right making me braver. "Just say it."

"Ok. I'm sorry," Cullen says. "There. How's that?"

I can tell by how uncomfortable he is that he isn't someone who is used to having to apologize, at least not at work. He probably isn't used to making mistakes and if he does, I don't suppose many people out right ask him about his attitude to them the next day. I am well aware that I could drag this moment out, ask him what he's sorry for, make him say it. I could lord it over him, tell him I told you so. But I don't do either of those things. He's still my boss and technically he didn't even have to tell me about this, let alone apologize, but he has done the right thing, the noble thing, and I won't throw that back in his face by being a bitch about it.

"Perfect," I say. "Apology accepted."

Cullen smiles at me and then his handsome face turns serious.

"Come for a drink with me. Now," he blurts out.

I feel like it's a question, but he words it like an order. That doesn't mean I'm going to follow it though.

"I don't think that's a good idea," I say.

"Why not?" Cullen challenges me. "Do you think after a drink you'd be unable to resist me?"

He grins and I laugh softly despite myself. I shake my head.

"It's not that," I say. "It's ..."

"It's two colleagues grabbing a drink because one of them fucked up and wants to buy the other a drink. That's it. One drink. No strings attached," Cullen interrupts me.

When he puts it like that, I can't think of any reason to refuse to join him and what harm can one drink really do? Even if I do find him irresistible, it's not like I'm going to jump on him in a bar.

"Ok. One drink," I say.

"Great," Cullen says, flashing me a smile. "Grab your stuff and meet me at the elevators."

I nod my head and then I leave his office and go to my desk. I put my jacket on and collect my purse and then I make my way to the elevators. Cullen is already standing there and when he sees me approaching, he presses the call button for the elevator.

It pings its arrival as I come up beside Cullen and the doors ping open. Cullen gestures for me to enter first and I step into the elevator car, and he follows me without a word. The sexual tension between us is thrumming as Cullen hits the button for the lobby and the elevator starts to go down. I wonder briefly if he's going to kiss me. I know if he does that then I should resist him, not let him know how easily he can get me to bend to his will, but I know that I won't do that. I don't think I would be able to resist his kiss even if I wanted to. It doesn't matter. The elevator reaches the lobby of the building, and the elevator doors ping open, and Cullen hasn't kissed me, although I did catch him looking at me with a lustful look on his face. He looked away quickly when I caught him, but I'm pretty sure he looked back in time to catch me smiling and biting my lower lip.

We cross the lobby and leave the building and I stand at the side of the cross walk waiting for a gap in the traffic so that we can cross the street.

"Where are you going?" Cullen says.

I look back at him to see him frowning at me.

"I thought we were going for a drink," I say.

The bar everyone in the firm uses for after work drinks is across the street and half way down the block.

"We are," Cullen says. "But if it's all the same to you, I would rather go somewhere that isn't full of my staff where I will only end up talking shop."

"OK," I agree, biting my lower lip again, this time to stop me from smiling.

Cullen has been to that pub plenty of times and he isn't

usually in the least bit put off by being surrounded by the staff or talking about work. He wants to be with me; just me. I feel like I am heading further onto dangerous ground but what can I do? Insist we go somewhere he's said he doesn't want to go? Tell him I've changed my mind? I don't do either of those things. Instead, I head into the danger. You only live once, right?

I follow Cullen and he leads me around the building to the parking lot.

"I'll follow behind you in my car," I say.

I don't know if he was planning that or if he thought I would be travelling with him, but I'm determined to stick to only having one drink and it will be easier to stick to that if I know my car is outside. He doesn't argue about it, he just nods his head in agreement, and we get into our separate cars, and I follow him as he pulls out of the parking lot.

Chapter 12

Max

I pick up my glass of white wine and sip it, enjoying the cool crispness of it on my tongue. The bar Cullen has chosen is nice. The lights are dimmed enough to make it feel cosy and intimate but not enough to make it feel like a dive bar. The music is soft and modern, and the chairs and carpet look clean enough to be new. The lights in the ceiling give off a soft yellow glow and the clientele seem similar to Cullen and me – city professionals having a drink after work.

"So, is this your local when you're not in the usual work's place?" I ask.

"I wouldn't really say it was my local. Me and my friends tend to meet here for a few drinks on a weekend before we go into town," he says. "It has a very different vibe on a weekend when everyone is in party mode rather than unwind after work mode."

I nod my agreement. I am sure the music will be louder, the people more raucous. It makes me wonder how the place looks so clean though.

"Where do you tend to go on a weekend?" Cullen asks. "Before you go clubbing, I mean."

I almost ask him how he knows I go clubbing, but I stop myself just in time when I remember exactly how he knows about that.

"We tend to hit a few of the cocktail bars in town," I say. "Or often we all meet at one of our apartments and have a pregame there and then just go directly to the club."

"I always feel like that's a good idea, but I know by the time midnight rolled around and the clubs would be livening up, I wouldn't be bothered to go if I wasn't already out," he says.

"It tends to work the other way with me," I say. "By the time it's time to go, I can't wait to get out and hit the dance floor."

We exchange stories about some of the times we've been out clubbing. Funny and embarrassing stories, stories of the best nights we've had, that kind of thing. Time flies as we chat and when Cullen excuses himself to go to the bathroom and comes back with another round, I don't complain. We keep talking, moving on to our families.

Cullen tells me about how his father died when he was barely four years old and how his mom worked her ass off so that him and his older brother, Liam, never went without anything. When he speaks about his mom and his brother, he changes, softens. It's clear he adores his family and it's nice to see this softer side to him.

He asks me about my family, and I tell him about my own mom and growing up with a single mom, although mine is because my dad was a dead beat who left her when she was pregnant. Cullen gets angry about this on my behalf, and I can't help but feel a glow inside at his protectiveness.

"It never really affected me, not having a father around. My mom made sure it didn't and that I didn't want for anything," I say.

"Yes, I feel pretty much the same," Cullen agrees. "I think it was harder for Liam, because he was seven when our father died, and I guess he remembered enough to know what it was like to have a dad where I was too young to really remember anything. I'm sure at the time I noticed he was gone and asked about it, but it wasn't something I carried with me in the way Liam did at first."

"In some ways though, I think it must be harder knowing you had a good father who cared about you and who died than just having a deadbeat who doesn't want you," I say.

"I think both are hard but in different ways," Cullen says. "And your dad is an idiot, because only an idiot wouldn't want you."

He looks into my eyes as he speaks, and his voice is low and gravelly. I feel a shiver of desire run through me and my pussy tightens. God he is hot when he does that whole alpha male thing. He holds my gaze and I squirm in my seat. I can feel heat flooding my face and chest and I know that my breathing has changed, coming in light little pants. I want him so badly in that moment that I know if he took me by the hand and led me outside, I would follow him home and let him fuck my brains out.

The tinkling sound of broken glass cuts through the pub and a quiet cheer goes up as the bartender drops and breaks a glass. The sudden burst of noise breaks the moment between Cullen and me and he looks away from me. I find I can breathe normally again, and I swallow away the remaining lust I feel for him. I won't let myself go there again.

"Another drink," Cullen says, starting to rise.

"No," I say. It comes out a little bit too loud and Cullen glances around before dropping back into his seat. I feel my face flush again, this time from embarrassment, but I press on. "I have to go. I said one drink and you already made it two."

"Third time's the charm," Cullen says with a grin.

I can't help but return his grin, but I shake my head.

"No honestly, I really do have to go. Thank you though, I enjoyed this," I say.

I put my jacket on as I speak and I get up quickly before Cullen can try to persuade me to stay, but I know that given the opportunity, he will try it, and I also know that I won't be able to resist him for much longer. It's hard enough now, but I won't give in. At the moment, I am the one in control here, the one with the power, but if I keep giving in, it won't be long before I end up getting hurt instead. I know I won't be able to stop myself from falling for Cullen if I keep letting myself hook up with him, and I know that's where this night will end up if I stay here any longer.

"Me too," Cullen says, accepting that he is beat. He stands up and takes my hand and kisses the back of it and then looks up at my face. "Next time I won't let you go so easily."

Goosebumps chase each other deliciously up and down my spine.

"Who says there will be a next time?" I say, my voice low and breathy.

"There will be a next time. Make no mistake about that," Cullen says, a wicked gleam in his eye as he smiles at me. "Good night, Max."

"Good night," I repeat and then I turn away and head for the door of the bar. It takes everything I have not to rush and not to look back, but I think I do quite well at nailing the casual saunter to the door, like I'm not affected by Cullen's statement, like I'm not dripping wet and like my clit isn't pulsing with need.

I step out of the bar and the door closes behind me and some of the hold Cullen has over me dissipates a little bit. I find that I can at least breathe normally, but my pussy isn't ready to let me get away that easily and by the time I reach my car and get in and start up the engine, I'm already planning on going home, getting straight in the bath, and taking care of the need for release that hasn't stopped building up inside of me.

Chapter 13
Max

I hold out my wine glass and Harriet tops it up with the last of the rose wine. This is our second shared bottle, and we have about an hour before our cab is due to take us to the club. I'm pretty sure I have some vodka we can drink that the wine is gone though so all is not lost.

"I wish I could get away with wearing a dress like that," Harriet says, nodding towards me.

I glance down at my outfit. I'm wearing a short white dress with cutout pieces on the sides and on the belly and back. The dress is essentially a bra top attached to a skirt by a few thin bits of material. I have paired the dress with silver strappy shoes with high heels and I'm wearing my hair down and wavy.

"You easily could," I tell Harriet. "You have a gorgeous figure."

It's true – she really does. I look across at her taking in her slim figure, her pert breasts, and her blonde curly hair. She's wearing a pair of black trousers and a red, plunge neck top.

"I just don't feel right in a dress. They aren't exactly me," she replies.

"You would get used to wearing them and then they would feel like you," I say.

Her cellphone rings before she can argue with me, and she glances at it.

"It's Sam. She was talking about meeting us in the club," she says.

"Cool," I say.

I haven't really seen any of my friends except Harriet since I moved, and I'm glad she talked me into going clubbing tonight and I'm happy to hear that I'll also get to see Sam.

"Our cab isn't booked for another hour," I hear Harriet say. She pauses and listens. "Shit." She looks at me and pulls the cellphone away from her face. "Sam is already in a cab. She thought we would be on our way by now. Can I tell her to come join us here?"

I know I should say no, but the alcohol and the rush of thoughts of our friendship have warmed me and made me less cautious, and I find myself nodding my head.

"Sure, but make sure she knows not to tell anyone where I live now," I say.

Harriet nods her agreement.

"Hey," she says. "Yeah, it's fine for you to come to Max's new place. Remember to keep the address private though yeah." She gives her my address. "The lock on the main door is broken so just come straight up. We're on the second floor. See you soon." She ends the call and turns her attention back to me. "You should really get on to your landlord to get that door fixed you know."

I snort out a half laugh and a half annoyed sigh.

"I wish it was that simple. My landlord owns this apartment and one of the others in the building, and the rest belong to several other landlords and none of them are willing to take responsibility for the door," I say.

"Well surely it's their joint responsibility and therefore they should share the cost," Harriet says.

"Well, that would be the sensible way, but one of the landlords insists he knows who broke it and it was nothing to do with his tenant so why should he pay? And then another one says his tenants aren't complaining about it so why should he pay? And then the rest of them, my own landlord included, refuse to pay towards the repair unless everyone does," I say.

"Oh God, what a shit show," Harriet says.

"Tell me about it," I say.

"Sam's taking her time isn't she," I say after a few more minutes pass by.

Harriet nods her head and drains her drink. She gets up and heads for the bathroom. I drain my own drink and go to the kitchen. I hunt through my cupboards until I find the bottle of vodka that I thought I had nestled away. It's three quarters full so it should last us. I grab a bottle of fizzy orange soda from the fridge and get an extra glass for when Sam arrives. I go back to living room with it all and I'm pouring myself a large drink when the front door opens and Sam bursts in.

"Let's get the party started," she says, and she whoops and holds up a carrier bag she's holding. It is almost see-through, and I can see the brightly colored test tube shots inside it.

"I stopped off for a few shots," she explains unnecessarily.

I get up and hug Sam and then sit back down and make her and Harriet a drink. Sam takes hers and has a big gulp. She grimaces.

"Jesus that's strong," she says.

Before I can ask if she would like some extra soda in it, she takes another drink and I figure it can't be that bad. Harriet comes back in and grins when Sam shows her the test tube shots. Sam gets the shots out of the bag and puts them on my coffee table and gestures towards them.

"Don't be shy," she says.

I grab a green shot and Harriet and Sam both go for blue. We open them and clink the test tubes together and then we take the shots. Mine is apple flavored and it's surprisingly nice although it burns my throat on the way down and I follow it with a big gulp of my vodka and orange soda.

By the time the next hour passes by, and our cab arrives, the vodka is almost gone. And the shots are completely gone. I'm feeling pleasantly tipsy and more than ready to dance the night away.

Chapter 14
Max

As I dance, I become vaguely aware of someone watching me. I look across the crowded dance floor and as my eyes meet a pair of beautiful dark brown ones, it's as if the rest of the club, hell the rest of the world, falls away.

Cullen walks towards me, his eyes holding me in place the whole time. He stops when he is within touching distance of me. He doesn't speak and neither do I. We just stare at each other, and I can feel my breath hitching in my chest. Cullen takes the last step and closes the gap between us. Before I even register his movement properly, his hands are in my hair and his lips are on mine.

I melt into his kiss, my lips moving with his, desperate for him to keep on kissing me like this. I wrap my arms around his waist and run my hands up his back, pressing him more firmly against me. I can feel his semi-hard cock pressed up against my stomach and I want him inside of me now. My clit pulses in time with the beat of the music and I kiss Cullen even more hungrily, moaning into his mouth as he strokes my cheek.

Finally, we pull apart and we stand looking at each other. I don't want Cullen to know the intense, dizzying effect he has had on me. At least not yet. I smirk at him.

"Stalker much?" I say.

"Dance with me," he says, ignoring my question.

I want to say hell no, he's not ordering me around like that, but the truth is, the command makes my pussy wet and I am powerless to do anything but let him take my hand and spin me around. I'm always aware of Cullen's body whenever we are in the same room together (and sometimes when we are not), but in this moment when we are moving together, I am hyper aware of his physical presence and how it makes me feel. My skin tingles and my lips crave his kiss. I find myself wrapping my arms around Cullen's shoulders and pulling his face down to mine. I press my lips against his and I relax my body against him when he kisses me back, his hands on my lower back.

Finally, we break apart and I notice a man standing to the side of us grinning in our direction. He approaches us now that we have finished our kiss.

"I'm guessing you must be Max?" he says. I nod, surprised, because I have no idea who he is. "I'm Liam, Cullen's brother. I'm the charming one."

I laugh a little bit and then it hits me that he knew who I was. That means Cullen has talked to his brother about me. Before I can really process that delicious little piece of information, Harriet and Sam are there too.

"Well, you're one step ahead of us," Harriet says to Liam. "Because this one has kept this very quiet." Now she turns to me where I'm standing blushing. "Aren't you going to introduce us?"

A look passes between Harriet and me and I mentally thank her for pretending like I haven't bent her ear a hundred times about Cullen.

"This is Cullen," I say. "And his brother, Liam. Cullen, Liam, this is Harriet and Sam."

Cullen smiles at Harriet and Sam and I swear Sam blushes slightly. I would be keeping a very close eye on her if it wasn't for the fact that she is already married to the love of her life.

"So, you're Max's boyfriend then I take it?" Harriet says to Cullen.

"Harriet. Jeez do you have to?" I hiss. This time the look I give her is anything but appreciative, but she pretends not to notice.

"What?" she says with a grin. "How else am I meant to find things out because you clearly forgot to mention we were meeting people tonight."

"I didn't know they were going to be here," I say.

I mean I hoped Cullen would be here – after all, we first met in this very club, and I had over heard him saying he was going out this Saturday – but I didn't actually know for sure he would end up here.

"I don't think they're official yet," Liam puts in. He flashes me a wide smile and winks. "Which is a good thing for me, because there's still plenty of time for her to see that Cullen here has a stick up his ass and choose the other brother."

"Back off Liam," Cullen says and although his mouth is smiling, his eyes aren't. He means it and I feel myself getting wet again at the possessiveness he shows towards me.

"Oh relax, I'm just joking," Liam says. "Now, who fancies a shot?"

That gets Harriet squealing and Sam nodding her approval and I shrug. Why not, right?

"Now Cullen, is it ok if I get Max a drink or are you going to go all caveman about it?" Liam says.

"Save your talking for at the bar," Cullen says with a laugh.

Liam laughs too and then he heads off for the bar and Cullen leads us to a booth style table at the side of the dance floor. He gestures for me to sit down, and I do, and I slide across and he sits beside me. Sam and Harriet slide in opposite me and when Liam comes back with the shots, Harriet squeezes down to make room for him, and I see her faint smile when his thigh brushes hers as he sits down. Interesting, I think to myself. I could see Harriet and Liam together. They would look cute together.

We all do our shots and I grimace as the heat burns my throat and spreads down inside of me. Laughing, I take a drink of my main drink – a bottle of Bud - to wash it away. The others seem to handle shots better than I do, none of them needing the chaser drink. Oh well.

Liam says something quietly in Harriet's ear and she giggles and then turns towards him and whispers her answer back to him. Cullen engages me in a quiet but flirty conversation that I am loving. His hand ends up on my knee and slowly, it moves higher, and I have to catch my breath as his fingers brush against the lace of my panties. He teases me, lightly caressing the lace, and then moving his hand back to my knee where it comes to rest.

I can hardly think, let alone talk, but I keep up my end of the conversation and I know the others don't suspect a thing. It makes Cullen's touch all the more delicious when it is a little bit taboo like this. God, I want him so badly.

His hand is moving back up my inner thigh when the music changes and Sam seems to come to life. I'm ashamed to admit I kind of forgot she was there.

"Oh my God," she squeals. "I love this song. Come on girls, let's go and dance."

She's up and pushing against Harriet and she and Liam have no real choice but to move. They all get up and Liam sits back down.

"Come on Max," Sam says.

"Leave her, she's all loved up," Harriet says with a giggle.

I kind of want to go along with that because right now, I can't imagine not being here with Cullen's hand on me and our bodies pressed together at one side. But I am not going to be that girl that ditches her friends at the first sign of some cock, and I already feel bad for forgetting Sam was here, even if she doesn't know I did that.

"I'm coming," I say.

"Not yet, but you will be," Cullen whispers in my ear. "We are not done here."

Chapter 15
Max

He stands up and smiles innocently at me as I slide along the seat to get up. My clit is throbbing with need and my whole body is alive and ready for Cullen.

"You're damned right we're not," I whisper to Cullen as I pass him and then I join the girls and we head back onto the dance floor.

I can't resist glancing back at Cullen as we walk and he's watching me and not even trying to disguise it. I can see the lust in his eyes from here and I feel my stomach roll with the anticipation of what's to come later on tonight. For now, though, I promise myself that I am going to focus on my friends and on having a good time with them and I throw myself into dancing. Even though I concentrate on my friends, I am still aware of Cullen's presence and his eyes on me as I dance, and part of me dances for him, wanting to turn him on and make him want me even more.

I know my tactic has worked when the bell sounds for

last orders at the bar and the lights come up on the dance floor and Cullen is there in front of me.

"Let's go," he says.

"Go where?" I ask, pretending to not know exactly what he means.

"My place," he barks out. "Now."

I can't speak. I can only nod my consent. Cullen takes my hand and leads me off the dance floor and then my senses come back to me.

"Wait," I say, gently pulling my hand from his. "I have to tell Harriet and Sam where I'm going."

I start back towards them. They are both laughing, and they come towards me.

"Go," Harriet says.

"Have fun," Sam adds with a wink.

I give each of them a quick hug and say my goodbyes and then I walk back to Cullen who takes my hand again, and without a word, leads me out of the club and down the stairs. I feel safe with Cullen, and I manage to get to the bottom of the stairs without falling or even stumbling. Cullen makes no comment on it, but I bet he notices. He notices everything.

He leads me across the parking lot and to the taxi stand, where he steers me to a waiting cab and opens the door and gestures for me to get in. I get in and he closes the door for me and goes around to the other side and gets in. He gives the driver his address and we pull away.

It's not that long of a drive – about twenty minutes or so, and they are twenty long, delicious minutes filled with the anticipation of what is to come.

I look out of the window as the city passes by. The

streets are quiet, but there is the odd house with a light burning in the window. I wonder if they are insomniacs or if they are people like Cullen and me who have been out clubbing.

Cullen's hand brushes mine where it rests on the seat between us and anyone else in the city, awake or asleep, goes out of my mind entirely as I feel tingles spreading up my arm from his touch. I turn my head and smile at him, and he licks his lips, sending a pulse of longing through my body.

Finally, when I'm almost delirious with the need for Cullen's hands and mouth to be on me, to have his cock inside of me, we turn onto Cullen's street and pull up outside of his house. Cullen pays the driver, and we get out of the cab and head through his garden. He unlocks the front door and pushes it open, standing aside so that I can enter. I go inside and I don't waste any time. I just head for the stairs. I'm halfway up them when the door closes behind me and Cullen starts up the stairs behind me.

"So eager," he says as he catches up with me at the top of the stairs.

I reach behind me and take his hand in mine, pulling him towards his bedroom, proving his assertion to be correct. I'm more than eager. I am ready to devour him and to be devoured in return.

We get into the bedroom, and I hear the door slam shut and I turn to face Cullen. We stand looking at each other for a moment, the air charged with static electricity that makes my body tingle. On some unseen cue, we come together in a flurry of kisses, caresses, and flying clothes. My hands roam all over Cullen and his hands roam all over me.

One minute they are in my hair, then he's cupping my face and then his hands are moving over my back and sides.

Once all of our clothes have been shed, I press myself against Cullen, feeling the hard muscles of his chest and his even harder cock. I want him inside of me, but there's something else I want to do first and when Cullen starts to walk me towards his bed, I let him lead me there, but when he goes to push me onto it, I slip out of his grip and shake my head.

"I want to taste you first," I say.

Cullen moans and pulls me to him. He kisses me roughly and then he turns us around so that he is next to the bed instead of me. He sits down and I pull my mouth from his and get to my knees between his legs. I take hold of his cock in one hand and direct the tip towards my mouth.

I lick lightly along the length of him and then I flick my tongue back and forth over the tip, tasting the salty goodness of his precum as I tease him. He moans again and takes my head in his hands, pushing the tip of his cock into my mouth. I let him move me and when he stops, I keep moving myself, taking his length into my mouth. I stop before he hits my gag reflex and I slowly slide my lips back up him. I suck hard on him and stretch his cock out then I plunge my head down, taking him into my mouth again. He moans again, a low sound that sends a shiver through my body.

I bob my head up and down, sucking on Cullen and moving my fist in time with my mouth so his whole cock is getting stimulated. I can tell by the way his breathing has become ragged and fast that he's getting close to coming. His hands are still on my head, fisted in my hair. It pulls slightly when I move my head, but I kind of like the soft sting in my scalp and I do nothing to encourage him to release his hold on me.

I keep working him, my head and hand moving, moving, moving. I'm loving the taste of him and the way he is slowly coming undone at my touch. My clit is pulsing, and I am so wet that I can imagine when I stand up there will be a puddle on Cullen's bedroom floor.

Cullen takes his hands from my hair and takes hold of my shoulders. He gently pushes me back and I resist him, still sucking on him. He pushes harder, his touch more demanding and I release his cock from my mouth, looking up at him questioningly.

"I want to come inside of you," he says, his voice low and almost a growl.

Another shiver of desire goes through me, and I stand up and Cullen moves backwards. I straddle him, wrapping my arms around his shoulders and kissing him on the mouth. I lift myself up and get ready to impale myself on Cullens swollen cock, but before I can do it, he flicks his hips and we roll, ending up with me on my back and Cullen between my legs looking down at me. I can see the lust in his eyes, and I know the look is reflected in my own eyes as I look at him.

"Twice now I have fucked you and then let you walk away from me. I won't be doing that a third time. If I fuck you now, you are mine," he says.

"I am yours," I reply in a breathy whisper, feeling my pussy clench.

"I'm serious Max," he says. "This is your last chance to walk away from this. From me."

"I'm not going anywhere," I reply.

Chapter 16
Max

Cullen studies my face for a moment, and then in one movement, he slams into me and fills me all of the way up. I cry out as he stretches my pussy and he slams into me again, deliciously relentless.

"You. Are. Mine," he declares as he fills me over again with each word.

I feel myself flood at his words. I swear I could come just hearing him say that without anything else going on. I'm not sure I fully believe he means what he's saying, but it's so fucking hot and I am more than happy to go along with it, although I hope he does mean it because I feel the same way – I can't keep doing this and walking away afterwards.

I moan and move my hips, needing to feel Cullen deeper inside of me. He obliges, filling me fuller than I have ever been and then he stops moving, holding me in place with his hips. He leans his head down to mine and runs his tongue lightly over my lips.

"Those lips? Mine," he says.

He kisses me, rough and hard and fast and then he pulls back.

"That mouth? Mine," he says.

He sucks on each of my nipples and tells me that they too are his. I am so close to coming now and my whole body is buzzing, desperate for release. Cullen has always been a good fuck, but this is next level good.

He finally moves his hips but instead of pulling back and thrusting into me again, he pushes forward, forcing himself even further into me. I gasp, feeling him against my cervix.

"This tight little pussy? All mine," he says. "Do you understand?"

I nod, desperate for him to start moving, to give me the release I crave.

"Say it," he growls.

"My pussy is ... is yours," I stutter.

He rewards me with a long, deep thrust and then he stops again.

"Just your pussy?" he says.

"No. All of me. I am all yours," I reply.

What starts off as a whisper ends in a scream as Cullen pushes his hand between our bodies and presses down on my clit as I speak. It is all the stimulation I need to go hurtling over the edge and I grip Cullen's shoulders pulling him down to me. He licks my neck and then kisses me lightly on the lips and then he starts to move, and he pounds into me again and again, dragging my orgasm out deliciously until I feel like I am just a giant nerve ending with no purpose except pleasure. My pussy tightens and relaxes and my clit pulses erratically, letting me I'm coming down from this intense high but then sending me peaking back up again.

I don't know how long that orgasm holds me in its thrall for, but it is still flooding through me when Cullen presses his face into my shoulder and comes with me. He slips out of me and my pussy clenches one more time and then I start to slowly coast down. I cling to Cullen, and he makes no effort to move himself off of me. I can feel the heat of his breath on my shoulder as he pants and the way he is struggling to get control of himself tells me that he came as undone as I did.

Finally, he rolls to the side and lays on his back beside me and I feel cold where his body has left mine and I feel empty where before I felt so deliciously full. Cullen pulls the duvet up over us, and I am no longer cold, but I still miss the feeling of his cock inside of me.

We lay side by side, still getting our breaths back. We don't talk, but Cullen's fingers find mine and that little bit of contact is nice and it's enough for me to know that while he probably didn't mean what he said while he was fucking me, that he isn't kicking me out of his bed right now either.

Part of me wants to ask him if he did mean what he said. At the time, he sure sounded serious when he growled out that I was his and that by fucking him one more time I was agreeing that I wouldn't walk away from him again. But surely. he was just talking from a place of lust. I want to ask him, but I'm afraid of the answer. He might say no, he didn't mean it, and I will be crushed, because despite myself, what I feel for Cullen is a lot more than just physical. It doesn't matter how much I tell myself that he is an asshole. He is an asshole at times, but he's my asshole and I love him for it.

My other worry is that he laughs at me for even thinking he might mean it. Maybe it's just his thing in bed, something he says to all of his conquests.

Yes, that's probably it, I decide. It hurts my heart to think like that, but I think it's better that I accept this now for myself than to have to have Cullen spell it out for me. I'm just going to act the way I always have with him and assume that the bedroom talk stays in the bedroom and doesn't have any bearing on our actual real lives. I don't like thinking of this, because it leaves an empty feeling in more than just my pussy and I turn my head to speak to Cullen about something, anything other than what is currently on my mind.

His eyes are closed, and his mouth is slightly open as he sucks in long, deep breaths. I smile to myself. I have worn him out. I watch him for a few minutes, appreciating how hot he is and how he looks younger with his face relaxed in sleep. I force myself to look away, not wanting my staring at him to wake him up. I lay in the darkness, thinking of anything but Cullen's words and it occurs to me that I'm not going to be able to sleep until I have emptied my bladder which is becoming uncomfortably full. I don't want to get out of Cullen's nice warm bed, but I want to sleep and so I know I have to. I sigh and sit up and then I get out of the bed and head for the door.

It's not as cold as I thought it was going to be, although my nipples seem to disagree with that as they swell and harden. I leave the bedroom and realize I don't know where the bathroom is. I try the door next to Cullen's room but that's another bedroom. The next door I try is the bathroom and I slip in and flip the light on. I close the door and use the toilet. I stand up and flush and then I look at myself in the mirror over the sink while I wash my hands.

I'm flushed and my eye lids look heavy, but I have never looked more alive. Cullen isn't just bringing my pussy to life; he's bringing all of me to life. I can't believe the man I thought I hated has somehow become the one man that I crave. I shake my head, smiling at the absurdity of the situation.

I shut the tap off, dry my hands, turn the light back off and leave the bathroom. I wait for a moment letting my eyes adjust to the sudden darkness. Once I can see again, I head back to Cullen's bedroom. I go inside and close the door as quietly as I can, but Cullen stirs at the sound anyway.

"I hope you're not trying to sneak out on me again Max," he says.

"I ... No," I say, walking towards the bed. "You caught me sneaking back in, not out. I went to the bathroom. I didn't mean to wake you,"

"Good," he says. "Because I meant what I said Max. You are mine now and that means you don't get to go sneaking away from me."

I nod my head, unable to speak in the moment. He lifts the duvet back for me as I reach the bed and I slide down onto the mattress and he covers me up. He holds his arm out to me, and I roll towards him, putting my head on his shoulder as he wraps his arm around my shoulders. I put my hand flat on his stomach and feel it gently rising and falling with his breaths. I hook one leg over one of his and he shuffles closer to me and rubs his fingers in a circle on my shoulder.

"You really meant it? That I ... I'm yours now?" I dare to

whisper, made brave enough to ask the question by the fact that he brought it up first.

"I meant it," he says. "And I hope you did too because I am not letting you go."

"I did," I confirm.

"Let me hear you say it then," he says.

"I am yours," I say without embarrassment or hesitation.

He kisses the top of my head.

"You are mine," he confirms, his voice starting to get thick with sleep once more. "And don't you ever forget it."

We fall into a comfortable silence and after a few minutes, Cullen starts to snore quietly. I close my eyes, but sleep doesn't come and take me just yet. This time though, I'm not kept awake by worry, or even by Cullen's snores. I'm kept awake simply because I'm delighted to learn that he really meant what he said.

I am his.

I try the thought on for size in the privacy of my own mind and I find that I like it.

I am his.

Yes. It feels right and I smile to myself. I'm still smiling when sleep finally takes me.

Chapter 17

Cullen

I wake up and smile when I see Max laying beside me. She is facing away from me, and her hair is hanging down her back. She has one arm out of the duvet. Even after the conversation we had last night when I thought Max was sneaking off, but she was really just on her way back from using the bathroom, I still half expected her to be gone when I woke up this morning. But she is still here, and I decide that she deserves a nice treat to wake up to seeing as how she has been a good girl and done as she was told to.

I put my arm around her waist and run my fingers over her belly and down towards her clit. She stirs slightly but she doesn't fully wake up as my fingers run over her skin. I press my fingers between her legs, opening her lips up and running my fingers over her clit. Max moans as I lightly tease her and then I apply more pressure and begin to move her clit from side to side. Max comes awake properly then, moaning louder and shifting position slightly so that I can get to her clit easier.

"Good morning," I say, and I kiss her neck.

"Good morning," she moans back. "I could get used to being waked up this way."

"I bet you could," I say.

I kiss along Max's shoulder bone and then back towards her neck. I nibble gently on the tender skin there and as I nibble, I increase the pace of my fingers on her clit. I bring her right to the edge of coming – I can tell she's almost there by the wet, warm rush over my fingers and by the way her breathing changes and her muscles start to tighten up.

I'm already rock hard and ready for her, and I pull my fingers away from her clit. She makes a noise of frustration and I laugh softly.

"Patience now," I whisper, making sure to let my tongue tickle her earlobe when I have spoken.

"Fuck me Cullen," she says, her voice barely above a whisper. So much for her being patient. But I get it because I can hear how full of need she is, and it would be rude not to oblige her I feel.

She starts to try to turn over, but I hold her in place with a hand on her hip.

"Stay right where you are," I command.

I feel the shiver go through Max's body and I smile at the effect I have on her. It's good to know she responds to me as much as I respond to her.

I move my hand off her hip and as instructed, she stays in place. I run my fingers across her bare ass cheeks and then I reach her pussy and run my fingers through wetness. We both moan – her at my touch and me at how wet for me she is already.

I push my hand between her thighs, and I lift her top leg

up into the air. I run my cock between her ass cheeks and down towards her pussy and when I reach the opening, I slam inside of her. She feels tighter than ever in this position, and I know she feels the effect too as she cries out as I enter her.

I begin to move, thrusting in and out of her tight little pussy, relishing the wetness of her and how she makes little whimpering sounds as I push her closer and closer to coming.

As I thrust into Max, I start to find the position we are in frustrating. For all it makes her already tight pussy even tighter which I like, it also means I can't quite get my full length inside of her because the angle is wrong.

I release her leg, staying inside of her and she cries out again as her legs close. I moan as my cock is squeezed deliciously and for a second, I stay there, relishing this feeling. I know I'm on the verge of coming though and I want to finish us both off properly and so I whisper to Max.

"Roll onto your front," I tell her.

As she moves her body forwards, I go with her, rolling into the gap between her now spread legs. I take her hips in my hands and fill her all of the way up, loving the sounds she makes as I fuck her. I lift her hips, pulling her up onto her knees and she sees my intention and pushes herself up onto all fours.

I look down and take in Max's delicious little ass and the sight of my cock disappearing inside of her, and it almost pushes me over the edge. I know I can't hold out much longer and I leave one hand on Max's hips. The other hand, I move around to the front of her body, and I push my fingers between her lips again and once more find her engorged clit.

It pulses to life beneath my fingers, and I work it in time with our now desperate thrusts and just as I realize that I can't stop myself from coming any longer, Max's pussy clenches around me and she calls out my name in a voice that is dripping with pleasure and I come in her, hard.

My orgasm slams through my body, making my already hard cock go even harder and making all of my muscles tense up. I try to breathe but I can't. I'm suspended in time, my eyes squeezed closed and my mouth hanging open as ecstasy stronger than anything I have ever felt before floods my body. I make a swallowing gesture although my throat and mouth are dry, and my face contorts in sweet agony as another wave of pleasure floods me. I spurt into Max again and I find I can move enough to pull her all of the back onto me, and I feel her pussy clenching around me.

I open my eyes and look down at Max. Her back is arched, her head thrown back. My orgasm finally begins to recede, and I can breathe again. I suck in a deep breath and then I gasp and pant, trying to get my breathing under control. I slip out of Max and her body relaxes and she slumps forward onto the bed. I lay down beside her. She stays on her stomach, her face turned towards me, and she gives me a lazy smile.

"If I had known you were going to do that, I would have stayed the last time too," she says, and I can't help but laugh.

I lean forward and kiss the tip of her nose.

"Only good girls get that kind of a wake up call," I tell her.

"Oh, and here's me thinking you like me best when I'm bad," Max replies.

I feel my cock start to harden again at her words, but I don't think Max is ready for another round yet. She looks like she's three quarters of the way back asleep and I can't help but notice her wince when she moves. I think her poor little pussy has had enough of me for now.

"Well at least when you are bad, I get to think up new ways to punish you," I say.

I spank her ass lightly and she whimpers but she grins at me, and I grin back at her. I push the duvet back, although I don't really want to.

"I'm going to go and grab a shower and then I'll make us some breakfast while you shower," I say.

"Sounds good. Wake me up when you're out of the shower," Max says and closes her eyes.

Chapter 18
Max

I get up and go to my walk-in closet. I go inside and select a pair of black boxer shorts and black jeans, and a white t shirt and a pair of black socks. I take them to the bathroom where I quickly use the toilet and then get in the shower. I blast the water out, nice and hot and soap myself up. I wash my hair and then I rinse myself down all over. I stay under the spray for a moment when I'm done, enjoying the feel of the water on my skin. Finally, I step out and dry myself off. I rub my hair and then I brush my teeth and run my fingers through my hair. I spray deodorant on and then I dress and shave and add a touch of cologne.

When I'm done, I wander back through to my bedroom where I push my feet into a pair of sneakers and then I go over to the bed to wake Max up. I debate shedding all of the clothes I have just put on and waking her up the same way as I did half an hour ago, but that would be such a waste of my shower and we have plenty of time for that. For now, I'm hungry for something else. Something like breakfast.

I sit down on the edge of the bed and gently shake Max's shoulder. She moans and opens one eye and smiles sleepily up at me.

"Are sausages and hash browns ok for breakfast?" I ask her.

She opens the other eye and sits up and nods her head.

"Perfect," she says.

"Ok. Go and shower or whatever you want to do and come down when you're ready," I tell her. "And there's a new toothbrush in the cabinet above the sink if you want to use it."

I kiss her forehead and then I hurry out of the room before the tingling in my lips can push me into forgetting everything but ravishing Max. I hurry downstairs and put a pot of coffee on and then I find the hash browns and the sausages and start gently frying them. They haven't long been in the pan when I hear the water start to run and I know Max is up and in the shower.

She times it perfectly. The coffee is ready and poured into two mugs and I'm just putting our food onto plates on the table at the end of my kitchen when Max comes in.

She is wearing last night's dress, but all of her makeup is gone, and her hair is damp around her face. I love her looking fresh faced and natural like that. If anything, she is even more beautiful without makeup on.

"What?" she says, her hands going to her face. "Do I have toothpaste on my mouth or something?"

"No," I say smiling and gesturing for her to sit down. She does and I sit down opposite her. "I was just thinking how beautiful you look this morning."

Max makes a snorting noise from her nose.

"The word you're looking for is rough," she says.

"You don't look even close to rough," I tell her.

She snorts again but she doesn't argue. Instead, she starts to work on her food, and I do the same.

"Do you have any plans for this weekend?" I ask Max after we have eaten in a comfortable silence for a while.

"Well, I didn't," Max says. She gives me a mischievous smile. "But now I'm thinking I might take you to the opticians see if we can get your eyes fixed."

I laugh and shake my head.

"I had something a little bit more fun in mind," I tell her.

"Oh yeah? Like what?" she says.

"Well, I thought we could go to the spa and get some nice relaxing massages and then spend some time in the steam room," I say.

Max thinks for a moment and nods her head.

"That sounds perfect," she says. "But I need to go home and change first."

"Oh, but you look so good in that dress," I tell her.

"I'm not sure it's exactly spa appropriate though," she says. That wicked grin I love to see on her face is back as she looks into my eyes and lowers her voice. "And I need to get some panties."

Her meaning hits me – she's not wearing any panties right now because she didn't want to put last night's back on – and my jaw drops. I feel my cock starting to harden and Max laughs softly at my expression. Oh, she knows exactly what she's doing, this one.

I get off my chair, the last bit of my breakfast forgotten. I come around to Max's side of the table. Fuck the shower. I can live with having another one. Max turns towards me as I approach her, but her smile fades, replaced by a wince of pain. I crouch down beside her, concern lining my face as I touch her shoulder.

"What is it?" I ask. "What's wrong?"

"I'm just a little bit sore down there," she says, flushing slightly.

"I hurt you?" I say, dismay settling into my stomach like a hot brick.

"No, not at all," Max says quickly. she cups my cheek with her hand and smiles at me. "My clit is just tender with all the overuse."

I smile back at her.

"Well then I guess I should kiss it and make it better," I say.

Max's eyes don't leave mine as she nods her head. I shift position so I am kneeling down rather than crouching and I push Max's dress up. She lifts herself long enough for the dress to skim past her ass and then she sits back down and scoots to the edge of the chair.

I gently open her legs and look at her pussy spread wide open waiting for me, but I can see she is red and somewhat swollen, and I vow to give her gentle oral sex and nothing else. I don't want her to be in any pain whatsoever. I lean forward and plant a gentle kiss on Max's tender clit. She sighs, a soft sound that makes me glance up at her because I can't read its meaning. Her eyes are closed, and she's got a faraway smile on her face, and I take it that means that the sigh was a good one. I move my attention back to her clit. I kiss it again and then gently and slowly, I begin to lick her.

I'm careful not to apply too much pressure and

although I desperately want to suck her clit into my mouth and make her come hard, I resist the urge. Just like I know I will resist the urge to bring her to the edge and then fuck her brains out. This isn't about me and what I want to do. It's about Max and showing her that I can be gentle with her when she needs me to be, as well as give her mind blowing orgasms.

I keep licking her, tasting her arousal. She tastes of salt and musk and very faintly of my shower gel. When I know she is close to coming, I know the gentle licks won't be enough to push her over the edge. I still don't want to be too rough on her clit and so I slowly lick my way back through her slit to her pussy.

I lap my tongue around the edges, licking up her juices and swallowing them down with an "umm" sound. I gently push my tongue inside of Max's pussy and she moans loudly. I move my tongue in and out of her, licking at her walls as I fuck her with my tongue. She writhes against me, pushing herself tighter to my face and she hooks one leg over my shoulder, holding me in place.

It's a struggle to breath, but Max is worth it, and I don't make any move to back away from her. Instead, I keep tongue fucking her until she grasps my head in her hands and moans my name and I get a coating of her juices on the lower half of my face.

Max's body tenses, her pussy tightening on my tongue, and she moans again and then her muscles relax and her pussy's grip on my tongue loosens, and I pull it out of her. She takes her leg down from my shoulder and I move my face away from her pussy, but she still holds my head in both of her hands, and she hugs me to her stomach for a moment before she releases me, and I stand up. I smile down at her.

"Better?" I ask.

"Much better," she confirms.

She smiles at me and then she pulls her dress down, pulls her chair back to the table, and goes back to eating her breakfast like nothing has happened. She will never fail to amaze me, this girl.

Chapter 19
Max

After we finish eating, we head out to my car, and I drive us over to Max's apartment building so she can get sorted to go to the spa.

"My building's parking lot is your next right," Max says.

I put my blinker on and make the turn and park my car. We get out and walk around to the front of the building. Max pulls the door open and steps inside and I follow her.

"Shouldn't that door be locked?" I ask her.

"Oh, don't go there," she says, rolling her eyes. "It should be, but the lock hasn't worked since I moved in and none of the landlords are willing to take responsibility for it. I'm just glad I don't live on the ground floor."

"Yeah, I can't imagine anyone on the ground floor feeling too safe," I agree. "Do you want me to get onto your landlord and get this sorted out for you?"

Max shakes her head.

"No, honestly, it's fine. This estate is pretty quiet and it's not like it's obvious the lock doesn't work," she says.

She has a point there that only residents and their visitors would know that the lock doesn't work, so I let it go although I still don't really like the idea of her being vulnerable like this. I follow her up the stairs and to her apartment, where the lock at least works. She opens the door and I follow her in, closing it behind me.

Her door opens onto a fair-sized open plan living room, dining room and kitchen. Max nods towards a comfortable looking couch.

"Make yourself at home while I go and get changed," she says.

I go and take a seat on the couch and while I wait, I decide to call ahead to the spa and book us a massage each and then a private sauna room for after wards. I finish my call and sit and wait. I look around and spot a bookcase beside a window. I make my way over to it so that I can look closer. On the top shelf, a plant sits, and I'm impressed to see it is very much alive. Dotted across the shelves are various ornaments and knickknacks and of course, books. I scan the titles, smiling when I see a few I have also read and enjoyed.

I go and sit back down after a few moments of looking at the books and before long, Max reappears. She has changed into a pair of white shorts and a black halter neck top. She is wearing white sneakers, and she has put on a minimal bit of makeup and braided her hair back. She's switched her clutch bag from last night for an over the body black purse that seems like it would hold everything she might need for the week let alone the day. She smiles at me.

"Are you ready to go?" she asks.

I nod and get up and we head back down to the parking

lot. As we make our way down the stairs, I confess that I had a closer look at her books.

"That's ok," she says. "When you showered at your place, I read your journal."

"Do I look like someone who keeps a journal?" I say with a smirk.

Max shrugs one shoulder.

"I don't know. What does someone who writes a journal look like?" she teases me.

"I have no idea, but I don't have a journal and I never have," I say.

"Ah you're no fun," Max says laughing. "So did you spot anything on my bookcase that caught your interest?"

"I spotted Lord of the Rings," I tell her. "That was one of favorites growing up. And I was suitably impressed that your house plant is thriving."

"Do you want to know my secret?" Max says. "To how I keep the plant going strong?"

I'm the sort of guy who could kill a cactus, something that's rumored to be almost impossible to do and so I nod my head. We have reached my car, and we get in and I start the engine and leave the parking lot as we chat. Max smiles at me.

"I only buy artificial house plants," she says.

"You mean it's not actually alive?" I say.

"Got it in one," she laughs, and I laugh with her and shake my head.

Chapter 20
Max

I feel like a drowsy, happy sloth. My muscles have all turned to liquid and I feel so relaxed I'm almost convinced that I could float away on the gentlest of breezes. I can still smell the citrus tang of the oils the masseuse used on my skin. It's a fresh, vibrant scent, and I find it energizing mentally, despite my body's refusal to be energized in this moment.

My massage was amazing, one of the best I have ever had. The lady who completed it was so tiny I didn't think she would have the strength to do a nice, deep massage, but I was wrong about her. Once she got going, she worked knots out of places I didn't even know could knot up.

The massage finished about five minutes ago and although she reassured me that I should relax and take my time, I'm still kind of conscious of the fact she probably needs the room for her next appointment. Plus, I still have my sauna with Cullen to look forward to.

I roll onto my back and force myself to sit up. Once I am sitting up, I still feel relaxed, but the drowsiness wears off quickly and I stand up and now I find that I do feel ener-gized. It's strange how just sitting up could change the way I feel so much, but I'm not complaining. I feel absolutely great. I grab the fluffy white robe I was handed as I went into the locker room and put it on and leave the room.

I wander down the immaculate white hallway until I come to a sign pointing me in the right direction for the sauna. I follow the sign and come to a door which I open. A staffed reception desk is opposite the door and the lady there smiles at me as I enter.

"Good morning," she trills happily. "Do you have a booking?"

"Umm, yes, I think so," I say. "My partner booked us in so it's probably in his name. Cullen Monroe."

I feel a rush of warmth when I describe Cullen as my partner. It feels slightly alien but in the best way imagin-able. The woman doesn't bat an eyelid at the description – why would she? I don't know, but I kind of expected her to for some weird reason – and she looks at her computer monitor.

"Oh yes, there you go. You're in sauna three. Mr Monroe is already inside," the woman says, still smiling.

"Thank you," I say.

I take an uncertain step away from the desk and the woman seems to realize I don't know where I'm going.

"Just follow the hallway around. The doors are all numbered," she tells me.

"Thank you," I say again, and when I start moving again, my steps are more assured.

I find sauna number three with no incidents, and I open the door. A small entrance way, again all white and immaculate, greets me. There is another door leading off it and beside that door are two hooks. On one of them, a white robe already hangs. I am suddenly nervous. I have never been to an upscale place like this, but from everything I know of them – admittedly from the TV and movies – no one gives a shit about nudity, and I'm clearly expected to leave my robe here. I can't say I'm entirely comfortable with everyone in there seeing me strutting along naked, but I didn't bring my towel along and I think I will stand out more going in with a robe on than I will do if I am naked.

I open the belt, take a deep breath and slip the robe off and put it on the hook beside the other one. I pull the door open quickly and step inside, resisting the urge to cover my breasts with my arm and my pubic area with my other hand. I soon relax when I see that the sauna is small and contains only one person – Cullen.

He smiles at me through the steam, and I go and sit down beside him, glad now I didn't bring my robe in. I would have felt so stupid if I had.

"I thought it would be bigger than this," I say as I sit down beside Cullen.

"There are a couple of big ones, but the little ones are private, and I wasn't sure how you would feel about a communal sauna," Cullen says.

I almost lie and tell him it would have been perfectly fine. I don't want him to think I'm some sort of prude, but at the same time, if I lie and say that and we ever come here again, he will book the communal sauna and I'll have to pretend to be all chilled out and confident about it.

"I'm not sure myself," I admit. "I've only ever been to

the sauna once or twice and it was ladies only. I like this private one a lot though."

"I'm glad you like this," Cullen says and smiles at me. "I usually go in the communal one, but I must admit I am never one hundred percent comfortable in it. But let's be honest, booking a private sauna on your own is kind of weird isn't it."

I laugh and nod my head.

"Yeah, it kind of is," I agree.

Cullen leans forward and picks up the jug of water and pours some of it onto the hot coals. They hiss and sizzle and a cloud of steam pours off them and the temperature in the room lurches up. I lean back on my hands and turn my face upwards and close my eyes. I sigh in contentment.

After a few minutes, there is another hissing sound and again, it gets hotter. I can feel the sweat standing out on my skin, and I relish the caressing touch of the heat. A moment passes and I realize that the heat isn't the only caressing touch I can feel now. Cullen is running his hand over my nipples, teasing them into hard little points. I go to open my mouth and tell him not to do that here, but I am warm and relaxed, and I don't have the energy to resist him. It's a private sauna after all. It's not like anyone else is going to come in.

He takes his hand away from me but before I can express my disappointment, I feel his warm lips on my neck. He kisses it and then he runs his tongue up it, tasting my sweat. He kisses down it again and then he keeps going, his mouth getting lower until he sucks one of my breasts into his mouth. He flicks his tongue back and forth over the nipple sending intense shocks through me. My nipples seem to be extra sensitive in here and I love it.

Cullen cups my other breast in his hand and kneads it while his tongue continues to tease the one in his mouth. Finally, he releases my nipple and my breast, and then he swaps them over, taking the other one in his mouth and the now damp one in his hand. He has me on the verge of coming when he slips his mouth off my breast and kisses down my stomach. He runs two fingers though my slit and my body responds to him as always – spreading my wetness over his fingers.

I'm still a little bit tender down there, but I'm nowhere near as sore as I was over breakfast, and I am more than willing to take a little bit of pain to get to the pleasurable part. I open my legs wide, willing Cullen to go further down with his kisses.

He obliges without me speaking, but not in the way I had in mind. He skips my pussy completely and kisses his way down my inner thigh and then he kisses his way back up the other one. He repeats this and although it feels amazing, I need to feel his mouth on my more sensitive parts.

"Cullen please," I moan.

"Please what?" he asks, his mouth still on my thigh, his breath tickling my skin there.

"Higher," I say. He doesn't move and I know he is going to make me say it. At least with the heat in here, he won't see how much my cheeks will burn as I do. "Eat my pussy."

He pulls his head away from my thigh altogether.

"Are you sure that's a good idea Max?" he says. "There are security cameras in here you know."

My eyes fly open, and simultaneously, my legs fly closed.

"What? Why didn't you say so sooner. Oh my God," I say, cringing at the fact I sat there with my legs wide open while Cullen kissed my thighs. And what he did with my breasts. Oh God. I never really understood when people said they wanted the ground to open up and swallow them, but I get it now.

"I didn't think you'd mind," Cullen says.

"You didn't think I'd mind? Are you shitting me?" I almost screech.

"Yes," Cullen says.

"Huh?" I reply, his one word answer catching me off guard.

"Yes," he says again, and he grins at me. "I'm shitting you. There aren't any security cameras in here."

I feel relief flood me and I laugh and swat at Cullen's arm.

"You bastard," I say, laughing now. "You really had me there."

"I couldn't resist it," Cullen says, also laughing. "Your reaction was priceless."

Cullen is still in front of my legs and as our laughter subsides, he gently pushes them apart again. I allow him to open my legs and he shuffles forward, and he moves his face closer to me again. He licks me between my legs, and I moan, more than ready for him to finish what he has started. He licks all the way through my slit again and then he centers his focus on my clit. I close my eyes again and lean back to enjoy this. Cullen massages my clit with his rough tongue, sending tingles through my body. He doesn't hold back or tease me this time, he just licks me until I come, hard.

Fire floods through me and my skin fizzes as pleasure sweeps through me once more. I make my hands into fists at my sides and moan as the pleasure radiates through me. It begins to recede, and I open my eyes and see that Cullen is no longer between my legs. He is sitting beside me again, his body coated in a sheen of sweat, his cock hard and at attention. He sees me looking at his cock and grins.

"Do you see what you do to me Max?" he says.

"I haven't even gotten started yet," I say.

Chapter 21
Max

I stand up, pour the last of the water out of the jug onto the coals, and then I straddle Cullen as the air fizzes around us. I slip him inside of me quickly before I can change my mind. He looks shocked, but good shocked and he makes no move to stop me as I begin to move up and down on his huge erection. His hands roam over my body as I move on him, long, slow strokes that fill me all of the way up and tease us both.

When Cullen can't stand the teasing anymore, he takes my hips in his hands and begins to move me up and down on him faster. He bucks his hips beneath me, and I work with him, moving faster and faster, my hands on his shoulders. I come a second before he does and we cling to each other, our hearts pounding, our breaths ragged and our moans low and full of almost pained pleasure.

I have just climbed off Cullen when there comes a sound like a doorbell. Bing bong. Then a female voice fills the sauna room.

"Attention sauna number three," the voice says, and

horror fills me. There are cameras in here after all and now this voice is going to tell us we are dirty and disgusting and turf us out. The thought should horrify me, and it does, but I can't deny that it also sends a shocking pulse of lust through me too. "Your time will end in approximately five minutes."

I giggle as relief floods me again and Cullen looks at me questioningly.

"I thought there really was security cameras in here when I heard the voice. I thought we were going to get kicked out," I admit, and Cullen laughs too.

"Are you ready to get out of here?" he says, and I nod my head.

Cullen stands up and holds a hand down to me. I take his hand and he kisses the back of mine and then helps me to my feet. We leave the sauna and go into the entrance room. I'm instantly aware of the cool air wrapping itself around me after the heat of the sauna. I snuggle quickly into my robe.

"I was going to ask you if you are brave enough for the plunge pool," Cullen says. "But judging by how quickly you got into that robe, I'm guessing it's a no?"

"Not a chance," I laugh. "A warm shower is more my jam."

When Cullen has his robe on, we leave the room and go our separate ways, me heading back to the locker room for a hot shower and Cullen heading to the plunge pool to torture himself. Before we part, we agree to meet back in reception.

I hurry back to the locker room and see that I have it almost entirely to myself. There is one other lady using the hair dryer and that's it. There are around ten shower stalls, so I take my time and enjoy the shower. I take my braid out and wash my hair again with the complimentary shampoo and conditioner, because now I have been all sweaty it feels kind of icky.

When I'm done, I step out and wrap myself in a towel from the rack. I go back to the section of the bench where my locker is and dry off and then I slip the robe back on and go and dry my hair. The other lady has finished at the bank of hair dryers which I am pleased about because it would have felt a bit awkward sitting beside her.

I dry my hair quickly and then I redo my braid. I stay in place at the hair dryer, and I use the mirror there to watch myself apply mascara and lip gloss, the only makeup I have in my bag, and then I go back to my locker again and pull my clothes out and get dressed. When I'm fully ready, I look around for somewhere to put the towel and the robe and I see a flap in the wall marked laundry. I figure that's the place and so I deposit the robe and towel down the chute and go out of the locker room. I make my way to reception and sit down to wait for Cullen. He isn't far behind me, and I stand up when I see him coming. He looks fresh faced and revitalized, and I feel like that too, so I hope I look as good as he does, as radiant.

He pays the bill and then we head towards the door.

"I have a plan for lunch," Cullen says. "Before I tell you, do you want a healthy chicken salad and a green juice, or burger, fries and a milk shake?"

"The second one," I say without hesitation.

"Thank fuck for that," Cullen says.

He leads me past the snack bar where presumably the

chicken salad and green juice would have been served. We leave the building and go back to Cullen's car.

"There's a place not far from here. It's kind of like a beach, except it's on a river rather than the sea, but there's sun, sand, and seclusion. I thought we could eat there?" Cullen says.

"That sounds great," I smile.

"There's a burger van just near the river where we can grab lunch," he says. "And don't worry. It's not a health hazard or anything. In fact, their burgers are better than any I've had in gourmet restaurants."

"I have nothing against street food," I smile.

"That was delicious," I say after I swallow the last bit of my burger. The fries are long gone but I still have my milkshake which is as good as the burger and fries were.

"I told you it was good, didn't I?" Cullen says and I smile and nod my head.

He was right about the food, and he was right about this spot. It's deserted, like our own private little beach and although the air doesn't smell of salt like at the seaside, it's as good as a proper beach. Maybe even better because a proper beach would never be this private.

"Can I ask you something?" Cullen says out of the blue. I nod my head and he carries on talking. "I wanted to ask you the first day you started working for me, but it didn't seem appropriate then. Why do you get called Max? I've tried every which way to get Max from Lucy or Granger and I can't do it."

I laugh softly.

"You'd have been there a long time," I say. "It's not off Lucy or Granger. When I started kindergarten, there was another Lucy in the same class and it got confusing I guess and rather than call us Lucy One and Lucy Two, our teacher started calling us by our middle names. So, I became Max off Maxine, and the other Lucy became Anne. It stuck with me all through school and by the time I went to high school, it seemed weird being called Lucy. No one called me Lucy then or now except my mom. I only use Lucy at work because it's easier than having to keep explaining that Max is a nickname."

"I thought there was going to be some big embarrassing secret attached to it," Cullen says with a twinkle in his eye.

"Sorry to disappoint you," I laugh.

Cullen's expression turns serious, and he cups my face with his hand and looks deep into my eyes.

"You could never disappoint me," he says.

I smile at him, feeling warm inside at his words. He leans in and kisses me, but this kiss is different. It's not the desperate, hungry kiss we usually share, it's slow and sensual and almost lazy. It's a kiss of love rather than a kiss of passion and that's when I decide that it's ok to let myself fall for Cullen because it seems like he is falling just as fast as I am.

Chapter 22

Cullen

Three Months Later

I can't believe how well things are going with Max and me. In one sense, I feel like I have known her my whole life, and in another sense, I feel like every day I learn something new about her, something that makes me feel even more strongly about her. I love that I feel like I know her enough to be completely comfortable around her, but that she can also still surprise me.

While no one at work has directly asked me if we are dating, I'm sure there will be gossip about it, because people have most likely noticed that Max and I have lunch together every day now. To be honest, I don't mind if everyone does know – it's not like we're doing anything wrong, and while the idea of a dirty little secret is quite a turn on, this isn't a secret, dirty or otherwise. The only reason I haven't actively told people at work is because it feels kind of like making a lame announcement to people because as CEO, no one asks me about my personal life really and I don't think Max has gotten close to anyone here, at least not enough for them to blatantly ask her if we're together.

At this point, Max spends more time at my place than she does at her own apartment. She has enough of her things at my place to get ready there and not have to go home to get a change of clothes or anything like that before work. Honestly, we are pretty much living together in everything except name.

I want to change that. I want us to officially live together, and I'm going to ask Max to move in with me. I've been thinking about it for a while now, but to be honest, I've been scared to ask her about it in case she thinks it's too soon and I scare her away. I don't really think that would be the case though. It's just my own paranoia speaking up, the part of me that thinks things are going almost too well and given the chance, I'm bound to fuck them up for myself somehow.

Max and I have just come back from a weekend away. We went to the coast and spent a weekend in a beautiful little beach house. It sat right on the beach and our back door opened onto our own private stretch of sand. We got up early the first morning and wrapped ourselves in blankets and went and sat on the sand and watched the sun come up. In hindsight, that would have been the perfect moment to ask Max to move in with me, but of course I bottled it and now I'm left needing to find something romantic enough to top that moment so that I can ask her.

Of course I could just ask her any time. I don't think the setting will affect her answer one way or the other, but Max is special, and she deserves the best and I don't want to just give her an effortless standard question. I want to wow her and make her see that I am worth moving in with.

As I'm thinking about this, my desk phone rings, and I smile to myself when I see it's an inside line and I know it's Max. I pick up the receiver.

"Why hello there oh light of my life," I say. "What can I do for you on this beautiful day?"

Max laughs and then she turns serious.

"I've just had a call from the main reception desk. There's a man there asking to see you. He doesn't have an appointment, but he was apparently very insistent that you would want to see him anyway because he has some news or something. He said his name is ..." I hear the sound of some paper rustling while Max gets the man's name from wherever she has jotted it down while on the line to the main reception desk and then she's back. "Derek Wellman. Should I tell them to make an appointment for him or just have them send him away?"

Derek Wellman was a guy I met when I first started the company. He was the liaison I had with a company I was doing business with and while I wouldn't say we were friends – we don't really know each other well enough for that – I would certainly say we were acquaintances, and we have a mutual respect for each other. For him to come to the office like this without an appointment, he must want something important, or he would have just called.

"Get them to send him up. I'll see him," I say.

"Ok," Max says, although she sounds uncertain, and I laugh softly.

How the times have changed. When she first started

working here, I would have taken that kind of response to mean that she was questioning my decision and then I would have snapped at her, telling her to just do what I was telling her to do and not make an issue out of everything. Now I realize that when Max sounds like she's questioning me, she is often questioning her own understanding of what I have said, and I know this is the case here because the instruction sounds off to someone who doesn't know my background with Derek. Now, instead of biting her head off, I quickly explain it to her.

"Don't worry I'm not going soft talking to any old crazy that wanders in off the streets. Derek and I go back a long way," I tell her. "I figure he wants something important to just drop in like this without making an appointment."

"Oh ok," she says and this time she sounds more normal. "Do you think I should move your three o'clock meeting just in case this goes on a while then?"

I check the time. It's only one thirty and I can't really see us needing longer than what time we have. Of course it really depends on what Derek wants.

"Leave it for now," I say. "I'll let you know if anything changes."

"Got it," she says. "I'll get reception to send Mr Wellman up now."

A few minutes pass and then there is a knock on my office door.

"Come in," I call.

The door opens and Max steps in and smiles at me.

"Mr Wellman for you," she says.

"Thank you, Lucy," I reply.

It feels weird calling her Lucy, something I only do in

front of clients and other members of staff. She nods her head to me and then she gestures for Derek to step into my office.

I stand up and go towards Derek and we meet in the middle of my office and shake hands.

"Would you like any refreshments sent in?" Max says.

I look questioningly at Derek, and he shakes his head.

"Not for me thanks," he says.

"No thank you," I tell Max and she nods her head again and leaves the office, closing the door quietly behind her.

"Take a seat," I say to Derek, gesturing to the chair opposite mine. "How have you been?"

"Good thanks," Derek says as he sits down. "How about you? It's been a while since we've talked, hasn't it?"

"Too long. I'm good too thanks. The firm is doing well and that's half of the battle, isn't it?" I say.

"Indeed," Derek says.

He doesn't elaborate further, and he seems to be waiting for me to say something more. I don't really know what to say except for to find out why he is here. We were never really ones for making small talk between each other and it seems like that hasn't changed.

"To what do I owe the pleasure of a personal visit then?" I finally say.

"I don't know if you heard, but I changed companies several years ago and I now work as an accountant for McPherson Financial Solutions," Derek says.

I hadn't heard that he had changed firms and I raise an eyebrow. McPherson Financial Solutions is one of the biggest and most prestigious finance companies in the city and they only take the best of the best to work for them, meaning Derek must be damned good at what he does. His working for such a company is news to me, but I'm not certain why he has come to tell me this now if it happened several years ago. Obviously, there must be more to it.

"You're wondering what that has to do with you," Derek says with a smile, and I nod my head. "I'm sure you can imagine the level of cyber security a company like ours requires."

I nod my head again. With all of the personal details they hold about their clients plus the actual money side of things, they are likely to need to be more secure than the FBI and the CIA put together.

"They've always done their own in-house cyber security," Derek continues. "But they've decided that it's become too much of a hassle to keep doing that and so they've decided to outsource it."

And that's where I come in and why he is here, I guess. Winning that contract would take this company to another level and we both know it.

"I recommended you to Mr McPherson and he told me to set up a meeting with the two of you," Derek says. "He's free tomorrow at ten or Thursday at three. Will either of those work for you?"

"Tomorrow is great," I say.

I have no idea off the top of my head what's going on then, but if there is something scheduled in, whatever it is, it can't be as big as this. If I do have something scheduled, I will either reschedule it or get my VP to deal with it. Either way, I am not missing out on this opportunity and the sooner I can get in to see the CEO, the better.

"Ok, give me a sec," Derek says.

He pulls a cellphone out and taps on it and waits for a moment until it pings and then he smiles up at me.

"That meeting is set," he says. "You must be wondering why I came here in person instead of just calling you."

"I am a little bit," I admit. "At first I thought it was because you didn't want the boss to know you were giving me a head's up but if he told you to arrange a meeting with me then obviously that can't be the case."

"We've always gotten on professionally and I liked the way you worked when you did work for my old firm," Derek says. "If this is going to be entrusted to someone on the outside, I can't think of anyone better than you for the job. And that's the honest truth. But I'm sure you know how much everyone in the industry is going to want this business." I nod again. Of course I know that. "Mr McPherson will take recommendations seriously – he likes to know that the people he works with are reputable – but ultimately, the bottom line is always the bottom line."

"The cost," I say and it's Derek's turn to nod his head.

"Got it in one," he says. "You need to not only give a competitive price compared to your competition, but you either need a good price compared to doing the services in house, or at the very least a solid pitch as to why the extra money spent will be worth it."

None of this is news to me. I know this industry and I know what I need to do to secure large contracts. And this still isn't explaining why Derek couldn't say that over the phone. His boss would hardly be angry at him asking me for a good price for him.

"You can keep quiet if you somehow found out something you perhaps shouldn't know right?" Derek asks.

I nod my head, intrigued where this is going.

"Good," he says. "I should be going now. If I happen to drop something on my way out, you should probably shred it. But have a good look at it first, just to make sure it isn't something I might want back."

I have no idea what he's talking about, but he stands up and extends his hand and the only polite thing to do at that point is to shake his hand. I'm starting to think he's gone a little bit senile, but then when he turns to leave, he puts his hand in the pocket of his suit jacket and pulls out a folded up piece of paper and lets it drop to the floor.

"Oops," he says, not stopping to retrieve the small piece of paper.

I don't know what the hell is on it, but I get what he meant now. I'm to see whatever is on that piece of paper and then shred it and not tell anyone about it. Ok, I can do that.

"Thanks Derek," I say as he reaches the door to my office.

"No worries. Hopefully we'll be working together soon," he says and then he is out of the door and gone. I get up and go and retrieve the sheet of folded up paper that he has dropped.

I sit back down at my desk and unfold it and my jaw drops. What he has given me is absolute gold. It's a full breakdown of everything Mr McPherson has in place security wise and a full costing of it all. I can use this to decide what is working for him, what isn't, and what else he needs plus I can even make sure that my quote is as competitive as it needs to be.

I call through to Max and tell her to clear my schedule

for the next morning and to clear her own too and to replace our morning with the McPherson Finance Solutions meeting. Once that is taken care of, I tell her not to disturb me unless it's urgent and I spend the next four of five hours putting a prospective offer together for the next day. When I'm done, I remember my promise to Derek, and I am a man of my word, so I go and shred the original sheet he gave me to work from. If we get this contract, I am going to owe Derek a serious favor.

Chapter 23
Cullen

"Fuck," I say.

"What's wrong?" Max asks me.

We arrived at McPherson Financial Solutions a little over ten minutes ago. The receptionist informed us that Mr McPherson was just finishing up something, but that we were to make ourselves comfortable and get ourselves and our equipment set up for our meeting. She has brought us to a small conference room with a table that looks like it would seat ten people comfortably, and all of the necessary equipment for a slide show stands at the front of the long table.

I haven't prepared anything like that at this point – this is more of a testing the waters style meeting, but of course I do have some charts and figures to show. I have set the laptop up and hooked it up to the screen and that has all gone well. But then I had taken out the other laptop I had brought; the one I wanted Max to use to take notes on.

"The battery is dead on the laptop for you to use to take your meeting notes on," I say.

I am so angry at myself for not checking the battery level before I had left my office.

"I'll use my cellphone," Max says.

"Will that work?" I ask.

"Sure," she says. "I can take the notes the same as I would on a laptop and then when we get back to the office, I'll just email them to myself, so then I have them on the computer to type up properly."

"Ok, yes, that's great. Do that," I say.

Max gets her cellphone out and taps a few buttons and she smiles.

"Actually, I can go one better. I'll turn the voice recorder on and just record the whole meeting and then it's just a matter of transcribing it rather than trying to put it back together from notes," she says.

"Even better," I agree.

She smiles at me, and I'm glad I brought her today. Originally, I brought her more because it looks more professional to turn up with an assistant, but now I am really glad I did it because she has solved what could have become a major problem for me.

After another five or so minutes, the door opens, and a man comes in. He looks like he's likely in his middle to late fifties and he has a neat grey beard and short grey hair. His eyes are blue and bright and alert and the way the man carries himself tells me he is someone important here and I think he is most likely Mr McPherson. He is wearing a tailored grey suit that fits him to perfection. He smiles at me and then at Max.

"I'm sorry to have kept you waiting. I'm Steven McPherson," he says.

I'm already on my feet as he speaks, and we shake hands.

"Cullen Monroe," I say, and then I nod towards Max. "And this is my secretary, Lucy Granger. Thank you for agreeing to see us."

"Of course," he says with a smile. "Please, sit back down."

I do as he asks, and he sits himself down across the table from Max and me.

"We're both busy people so let's not waste each other's time with pleasantries and platitudes. You come highly recommended to me, but of course I need to see for myself what exactly it is you're offering me," Mr McPherson says.

I like his no nonsense attitude and I find that there's something about him in general that I quite like. I think he would be a good person to work with, and my instincts for such things are usually spot on, a skill I have honed over the years, for the most part by ignoring it and ending up with clients who were more trouble than their business was worth to me.

I tap a key on my laptop and the screen on the wall springs to life displaying a list of things that I would suggest need to be included in a security package for the firm, and beside it, the cost for each individual item, with a total price at the bottom.

I spend the next ten- or fifteen-minutes talking Mr McPherson through each of the items on the list, explaining to him what it means in laymen's terms and then telling him why I feel that McPherson Financial Solutions should have it in place. Most of the items are straight forward enough and are already used in one capacity or another by the company, but some of their technology was older and I have replaced it with newer solutions and a couple of the things are new to the company altogether and those take a little bit more explaining, and Mr McPherson asks me several questions about those as we go. He seems to have a good understanding of the subject though which definitely makes my job here a bit easier.

I finish presenting my proposal and wait to hear Mr McPherson's thoughts on it. He takes a moment and then he addresses me honestly.

"That's all well and good and if I thought for a second there wasn't a catch, I would take your hand right now for this offer. But I am not a stupid man and I trust that you aren't either, so why don't you explain to me how much this package will actually cost me because that price is barely going to make you a profit," Mr McPherson says.

"It's not going to make me a profit at all," I say and smile at Mr McPherson's confused expression. "I'm going to be honest with you Mr McPherson."

"Call me Steven," Mr McPherson says.

"Ok, Steven it is," I agree. "I'm not going to be the only cyber security firm you talk to, and I know that the price is going to be significantly higher than what it would be if you were continuing to do your own in-house cyber security. I can sit here all day and explain the reasons why it is better to pay the extra and have experts take over the hassle of it for you, but every company will say the same things, and do you really have any proof that it's not just a sales pitch? So, I'm willing to put my money where my mouth is. We will come in and get set up and run it for three months at those prices. If you see the benefit of working with ITSafe, then from month four onwards, the price will increase by twenty percent, but by then, you will already know it is worth it and you won't be taking any gambles."

Steven looks at me for a moment and then he smiles.

"I must admit I like that concept. I like that you are confident enough to put your money were your mouth is," Steven says. "I'll need to discuss it with the board of course. Expect to hear from me within two weeks."

He stands up again and it's clear that we're being dismissed. Max and I take the hint and stand up too and Steven shakes both of our hands.

"Can you see yourselves out? I have another meeting in five minutes," Steven says.

"Of course," I agree. "I look forward to hearing from you."

Steven nods to me and he leaves the room. Max and I smile at each other and gather our things up and leave the conference room.

"I don't want to put a jinx on things," I say, once we're back in my car and headed back to the office. "But I really think that went well."

"Well?" Max says. "It went amazing. He would have said yes on the spot if it was solely his decision."

"Let's just hope he has plenty of influence over the board," I say.

We get back to the office and I pull up in the parking lot and Max and I head back into the building. We go up to our floor and I pause by her desk.

"I need the notes from that meeting typed up and to me by the end of the day," I say.

"I'm on it," Max says. "I've already emailed the audio

file over to the computer. You'll have them in the next few hours unless something more important comes up."

I don't know what she thinks could possibly come up that would be more important than this, but I trust her to manage her work load in order of priority and so I don't say anything, I just nod my head and then I go into my office.

Chapter 24

Max

I wake up to find Cullen laid with his head between my legs, his tongue on my clit. I love staying over at his place because of mornings like this where he wakes me up in the most delicious way imaginable.

I let him lick me, sending the stirrings of fire through me and once all of my senses have been well and truly awakened, I press myself tighter against Cullen's tongue. I feel him smile and for a second his tongue moves away from me.

"Good morning," he says.

"Oh yes, it most definitely is," I confirm.

I feel rather than hear his laughter and then his mouth is back on my clit and he's working it faster. I move my hips up and down in time with his licking of me, but he presses his hand on my stomach to keep me in place and he pulls his face back from me slightly again.

"You will come when I am ready for you to come," he says in a low growl that sends a pulse of desire through my clit and up into my stomach.

He goes back to my clit and this time, he doesn't just

lick it, he sucks it into his mouth. He presses it against the roof of his mouth with his tongue. It's a strange sensation, something new to me, but it feels really good, and I find myself twisting the sheet that covers the mattress in my fists to try to stop myself from moving and trying to get my release quicker. I know if Cullen catches me doing that a second time, he will draw this out even longer, and tease me until I can't take any more.

Cullen plays with me as it is, rolling his tongue back and forth against my trapped clit and then he releases it and gently nips it between his teeth. Even the gentle nip stings in such a sensitive area, but the sting is matched with an equal blast of pleasure, and as the two sensations collide, it feels absolutely amazing. I am so close to coming now that I feel like one more touch will set me off, but Cullen has other ideas.

He lifts his head right up and away from my pussy so that I can see his face. The bottom half of it is soaked in my juices.

"Remember, don't come until I say you can," he commands.

I love it when he commands me to hold myself back. I don't have the self-control to do it for myself, but I will always want to please Cullen and I can do it for him. My orgasms are always better when I'm forced to hold myself back first.

Cullen keeps his eyes on mine for a moment, and then his face disappears back down between my legs and his mouth goes back to my clit, and he slips two fingers inside of my pussy as he licks my clit. He rubs his fingers in and out of me, slowly at first, making sure to press down on my g spot as his finger tips pass it. I grit my teeth, fighting the urge to just give in and climax and I let Cullen continue to work his magic until I'm in a frenzy. I feel like if I don't come soon, I will explode.

"Please," I whimper, begging Cullen to let me come.

"You're pussy is mine," he says. He doesn't move his head far back this time and I feel his growling words vibrating through my clit. "You come for me and me only."

"Yes," I say, almost screaming it in my enthusiasm. "Yes. Only for you."

"Come for me now," he says and then he sucks my clit back into his mouth and presses down on my g spot with his fingers which have remained inside me.

I'm overwhelmed with the rush of sensations, and I don't know what to do except ride the waves of warm pleasure. The sensations radiate from my clit up into my stomach and beyond and the sensations from my g spot bounce around my pussy and up my back. My whole body is alive in ways I never even knew was possible, and my orgasm isn't just in my pussy or my clit. It's in my womb, my breasts, my neck, my inner thighs. Every part of my body really.

It even affects the inside of my body, stopping me from breathing or swallowing, not letting me do anything except lay there and take what Cullen is giving me. Just when I'm starting to panic because my vision is going black from the lack of oxygen and I think Cullen is pushing me further than I can go this time, he releases my clit from his mouth and takes his fingers out of me.

Cullen stopping working me doesn't end my orgasm, it just stops it from being more than I can handle. I'm still floating in the air above my body, light as a feather, floating on a wave of warmth and ecstasy and then I'm back in my body, and I can feel my muscles going into spasms. It's not just my pussy that is tightening and then relaxing. It's the muscles everywhere in my body, making me twitch and lifting my back off the mattress and throwing my head back.

Finally, I feel the release that I crave, and I'm floating back down to earth, and the pleasure is fizzling slowly away, leaving me sated and exhausted and shaken to my very core. I flop down on the mattress as my muscles relax and my back comes out of the arch it was forced into, and I gasp in breath after breath of delicious air.

Cullen is running his fingers over my stomach, trailing my juices across my skin. I have never been as wet as I am now. I can feel my juices running through my ass crack and drenching the mattress below me. That's what Cullen does to me. He makes me lose all sense of time and place and takes my body back to its most primal level. It's amazing and awesome and tantalizing and perfect and everything I ever wanted and more.

Cullen has stopped drawing on my belly now and instead, he is running his tongue over me, licking my stomach clean again. He licks higher, flicking his tongue casually over one of my hard nipples and then the other one. He licks up my neck and then nuzzles my ear and nibbles on the lobe.

"You are mine," he says and then he slams into me, his hard cock filling me once more and taking me almost instantly back to that place where I hover between coming and not quite coming.

He pounds into me hard, not holding back at all, and I

meet him thrust for thrust. He doesn't try to hold me back this time which is good because I don't think I would have been able to stop myself from coming this time, even for him. Stars of red and white light burst in front of my eyes as my pleasure receptors flood my system with ecstasy once more. I feel Cullen's body stiffen on top of me as he comes with me, calling out my name in a strangled sounding voice.

With one last thrust, Cullen's orgasm fades and he pulls out of me, and rolls off me, leaving me coming down slowly. I feel heavy and sated, my muscles warm and like jelly. It's a lovely feeling and I hate knowing that I have to get up and get ready for work any minute now. I feel like I could quite happily lay here and doze all day.

Cullen props himself up on one elbow beside me and he leans down and kisses me. I kiss him back, wrapping my arm around his shoulders. He pulls back before I am ready for the kiss to end, but when I try to pull him back to me, he shakes his head.

"Later," he says. "I have to get to the office."

"The alarm hasn't even gone off yet," I point out.

"That's because I shut it off before I went down on you," Cullen says with a smile.

"Shit. Cullen what time is it?" I say.

"Eight thirty," he replies.

"Eight thirty? We're never going to be there on time. It's ok for you Mr CEO but I can't just come in when I want to," I say.

"No, but you can take a half day off when the CEO says you can, and I am saying you can. Why don't you stay in the bed a little longer, chill out for a bit. You've been working hard, and you deserve a break," Cullen says.

"Would you have done this for Lisa?" I ask.

"Well not like this," Cullen says with a smirk, gesturing down at our bodies beneath the duvet. "But yes. When she did exceptional work, she got rewarded with a half day here and there."

"Ok," I say.

I'm not sure if I believe him or not, but I am still feeling so sleepy and I'm warm and comfortable and I don't want to move yet so I chose to believe him.

Cullen smiles and leans down and kisses my forehead.

"See you when you come in," he says.

I nod my agreement and close my eyes and I drift off back to sleep.

Chapter 25
Max

I wake up again and see that it's past ten am. I can't remember the last time I slept in that late on a work day without being sick and it's nice to have a little bit of time to recharge my batteries. Cullen said to take half a day and I know if I get ready and go straight into the office now, he will only send me back away and so I decide to take a nice bubble bath instead of a shower. I run the water hot and put plenty of bubble bath in it and then I get in and lay back and close my eyes.

I finally get out of the bath when the water starts feeling cool and I realize how long I've been in when I see the prune like wrinkles on my fingertips. I finish getting ready and then I make and eat a ham sandwich and then I head off for work.

The first thing I see as I approach my desk is a note off Cullen. I pick it up and read it and I smile to myself.

"Come to my office immediately when you get in."

That's what the note says and my clit tingles with anticipation. If Cullen had a work task for me, he would have written it on the note or emailed me. This isn't a work summons; this is more personal than that and I have a feeling that I might be going to get "punished" for being late. I am more than down for that. In fact, it would be a good way to get me to take half days more often and if that means I'm taking advantage of being the boss's girlfriend, well I'm ok with that.

Grinning, I pop the note back on my desk and head to Cullen's office. I tap on the door, simply because I don't know if anyone is in there or not.

"Come in," Cullen calls.

I open the door and go into his office, closing the door again behind me. He looks at me and he doesn't smile or greet me, but I suppose that's all part of the act. It would kind of spoil it if he was all excited and eager to see me. My clit pulses and my pussy is starting to get damp as I stand looking at Cullen. I can feel my nipples stiffening in my bra.

"Take a seat," Cullen snaps.

I head toward the seat opposite his, but I decide against sitting down. If I'm going to be in trouble for being a bad girl, then I might as well make it for more than one crime. I walk around to where Cullen is sitting and wrap my arms around him from behind.

"Have I been a bad girl?" I say, bending down to whisper in his ear.

I'm shocked when Cullen takes my hands firmly in his and removes them from around his shoulders.

"This is serious Max. Sit down please," he says.

There is no note of a playful tone in his voice and although he is ordering me around, it doesn't feel like the way he does it in the bedroom and instead of feeling turned on, I am actually starting to feel a little bit concerned. What have I done wrong? I have no idea, unless offering me a half a day was some sort of test which I clearly failed, but I really don't think Cullen would play games like that.

I walk around the desk, feeling stupid now as well as concerned. I sit down and force myself to look Cullen in the eye. I don't think I've done anything wrong and if I have then I will own it, but if he thinks I'm going to sit here and be apologetic for thinking he was playing with me then he is going to be very disappointed.

"I don't ..." he starts. He stops and shakes his head. "How could you betray me like that?"

Now I'm completely lost. It doesn't sound like I've fucked something up at work. It sounds almost like he is accusing me of cheating on him or something similar but I haven't so much as glanced at another man since Cullen and I got together, and I have no idea what he's talking about.

"I don't know what you mean," I say honestly.

"You can drop the innocent act Max," Cullen says.

"It isn't an act," I say. "I genuinely have no idea what you're talking about. I haven't betrayed you in any way."

"Are you really going to make me spell it out for you?" Cullen says.

"I guess so because unless you do, I will still have no idea what we're talking about here," I say.

"Does the name Bill Bryson mean anything to you?" Cullen asks.

I think for a moment and then I shake my head. If he thinks I'm cheating on him with this Bill Bryson guy, then he is very much mistaken. I don't even know who Bill fucking Bryson is.

"What about Cyber Safe?" Cullen asks. "Have you heard of them?"

I nod my head.

"Now we're getting somewhere," Cullen says. "Who are they?"

"One of the firm's competitors," I say.

"Correct," Cullen says. "In fact, they are the company's biggest competitor, and the McPherson Financial Solutions contract was going to ensure that we stayed heads and shoulders above them. And it still will, no thanks to you."

He is jumping from topic to topic, and I still have no idea what I am meant to have done. Cullen sighs and rolls his eyes.

"Ok, I get it. You want to know how much I know so you know how much to admit to. Well, I know all of it, but I'll play along," Cullen says. "Bill Bryson is the head of new customer acquisitions at Cyber Safe. Do you know what his job is?"

"No, because I don't know him," I say. Cullen doesn't say anything else, and I realize he is waiting for me to say more. I think for a second and try to answer his question. "But if I had to guess, going off the job title, I would say he is in charge of getting new clients for his firm."

"Ring a ding ding," Cullen says.

I'm starting to get annoyed with Cullen's attitude now. He has no right to speak to me like this as either my boyfriend or my boss. I'm close to snapping at him, but I know I have done nothing wrong and that gives me the moral high ground so I'm going to try and keep myself from saying anything rude at this point so that I can keep that advantage.

"Imagine my horror when I get a call today from Bill Bryson. Because we might be rivals, but Bill is like me – old school, and he likes to play fair. He told me that he got an email from you with the full proposal I put forward for Mr McPherson," I say. "Care to explain that?"

"I can't explain someone else's actions, but if I had to hazard a guess, I would say he is doing it to put you on the back foot and make you question who you can trust. That gives him the opportunity to sweep in and take all of the McPherson Financial Solutions business for himself while you flounder around wondering what happened," I say.

It's a bit close to the line of what I should be able to say to my boss and what not to, but he asked for my opinion, and he got it.

"Wow. You are brazen," Cullen says, shaking his head. "In a grudging way, I almost admire the sheer balls it takes to sit there and not only lie to my face, but to then have the sheer audacity to look angry at me."

"I still don't know what the hell you are getting at here Cullen so instead of sulking and making half accusations, can you please just tell me what the hell it is that you think I've done?" I say.

I have definitely crossed a line now, but I don't really care at this point. He has just called me a liar to my face, and he can go and fuck himself if he really thinks I would do what he seems to be accusing me of doing.

"Bill didn't lie about getting an email. He knew every detail of the proposal down to the price I was charging and why I was offering such a big discount. And he told me the email was sent from you," Cullen says.

"And you just believed him?" I say, shocked at that.

"Of course not," Cullen says. "I gave you the benefit of the doubt and told him to prove it. He forwarded the email to me and then I couldn't tell myself he was lying anymore after that. I don't get it Max. What did I ever do to you that would make you want to destroy me like that? I gave you a job when no one else would, and you sell me out like that. What did he offer you? Extra money? A company car? Better annual leave? What? And you know what? I couldn't have forgiven you, but I could have shrugged it off as it being business and some people can't be trusted. But you would have gotten inside information like that about the company without you worming your way into my bed as well as my office."

"Are you fucking kidding me Cullen? It's bad enough that you think I would leak company information to anyone, but for you to actually think I would seduce you just to play with you. What sort of a person do you think I am?" I say.

I keep my voice low, but Cullen must be able to hear the anger simmering below the surface because I can't control the shaky quality that it brings to my voice.

"I don't know anymore. I thought I knew you, but obviously I didn't know you at all. You know, you shouldn't be wasting your time working for me or Bill Bryson. You should be an actress because by God, you are good," Cullen says.

"It's easy to act innocent when you are innocent," I say.

"You know what? I'm done. You're not going to have the balls to admit to my face what you've done, so whatever, go and slither off and find someone who employs snakes, because you've shot yourself in the foot at Cyber Safe, they don't work like that. And you've certainly shot yourself in the foot with me. You're fired Max. Get your stuff and leave immediately. And get your stuff out of my house before I finish here today because anything of yours left behind will be getting thrown into the trash," Cullen says.

The anger fizzles out of me as Cullen's words register with me. I have lost my job and my boyfriend within the space of a minute, and I haven't done a thing to deserve either of those things. I try to swallow past the lump that's forming in my throat, but I can't, and when the tears leak from my eyes, I make no move to stop them. Cullen sees me crying and rolls his eyes.

"Save the water works for someone who hasn't seen through your bullshit," he snaps.

I have had enough. I am not going to sit here and be abused for another minute. I stand up, trying to muster together what little dignity I have left. I look down on Cullen as he remains seated, and I put my hands on the edge of his desk.

"One day you will find out the truth of what happened with this," I say. "And you will learn that I did nothing wrong. When that happens, and you see what you've thrown away, I hope it hurts you even half as much as it's hurt me."

Chapter 26
Max

With that, I turn around and leave Cullen's office. I make sure not to look back as I slam the door closed. I go to my desk and empty out my personal belongings and then I go down to my car in the parking lot. I put all of my things in the trunk and then I get in the car and leave the parking lot. After I have driven for about ten minutes, long enough that anyone coming or going from the office wouldn't see me, I pull over to the side of the road and let the flood gates open up properly.

I sob, my body shaking as I hiccup and sniffle. I can't believe that the same man who woke me up this morning by licking my pussy threw me to the curb not five hours later. I mean if I had done what he was accusing me of then yes, I would have gotten it one hundred percent and I would have deserved it. But I hadn't and the fact that he hadn't believed that I hadn't hurt the most of all.

After a couple of minutes of undignified sobbing, I force myself to get a grip of my emotions. I open the glove box of my car and fish out a packet of tissues and close the glove box. I use one of the tissues to wipe my eyes and then another one to noisily blow my nose. Finally, I pull down the mirror over the steering wheel and peer in it, licking a third tissue and using it to get the black smudges of make up off my face.

With that done, I slam the mirror back up into its place and throw the remaining tissues onto the passenger seat and then I take a deep breath. I put my car back in drive and pull out into the road and head for Cullen's place. It's going to hurt like hell collecting my stuff, but it's better than the alternative. Either Cullen will indeed get rid of everything like he threatened to do, or he will bother me until I go and get it and it will be so much worse having to do it with him there. At least this way, I can grab everything in private and not worry about crying again.

Because I'm sure there will be tears. Lots and lots of tears. God, why didn't I just trust the part of my gut that didn't like Cullen in the first place? At least if this had happened when I didn't like him, it would have just pissed me off rather than hurt me.

I arrive at his house and get out of my car. I go to the front door and let myself in, and the first painful pang gets me. It will be the last time I am able to do that. I push the sadness aside and begin to work my way through the house collecting up my stuff. There isn't much downstairs – a couple of DVDs and a book. Most of it is upstairs because it's stuff like clothes, makeup, toiletries etc. To be honest, if it wasn't for the fact the makeup is all Mac, Dior and Estee Lauder and cost me a small fortune, I would have just left my stuff behind, but if I am going to make the effort to collect my makeup, I might as well collect everything while I'm here anyway.

I go upstairs with the DVDs and the book and first of all, I go into the spare bedroom and retrieve the small suitcase I used to bring all of this stuff over in the first place. I go to the bedroom and fight the urge to cry when I smell the sex on the air. It is the smell of Cullen and me mixed together, and it is the last time I will ever smell it.

"No," I say out loud as tears tickle my eyes again. "Fuck this shit. Cullen did this not me and I bet he's not sitting in the office crying over me, so I'm not going to waste another second crying over him."

I nod my head to emphasize my no doubt empty words and then I focus on going about the room collecting and folding my clothes and then placing them in the suitcase. I grab my dirty clothes back out of the hamper and then I go through to the bathroom and collect everything of mine from in there too. I think I have everything, and I do a quick sweep to double check I haven't overlooked anything.

I'm glad I do that last sweep because I find my cellphone charger still plugged in on my side of the bed – except it's not my side of the bed anymore, its now just the side of the bed that Cullen doesn't sleep on. I wrench the charger out of the socket as though it has somehow been the thing to offend me, and I drop it into my little suitcase. The only thing I could think of at the moment that could make me feel even worse would be to get home and not be able to charge my cellphone when it needed it and know my charger had likely been thrown away.

I zip my suitcase up and look around the bedroom one last time. I suppose it was good while it lasted, and nothing good can last forever, or some equally mushy bullshit. Why can't it last forever? Other people seem to be able to find happiness and have their relationships last all of their lives. What have I done to deserve my car crash of a love life?

My first serious boyfriend abuses me and then the next one accuses me of all sorts of crap and tosses me away like trash without even considering there is something else happening here. God what's next? Will I end up dating a death row inmate? A serial killer looking for his next victim?

Fuck it. I'm going to be a lesbian. Except I don't fancy women. Ok, I'll just be celibate then. At least then I will literally have no one to blame but myself if I am not happy and fulfilled. Maybe that is the way forward. After all, it seems like that's what the universe wants for me and what the universe wants, it gets, so why even fight it?

I grab the suitcase and go back down the stairs. and I step out of Cullen's door for the last time. I debate leaving it open, but I decide against it for three reasons. One, it's petty as fuck and he thinks badly enough of me as it is without being able to add petty to the list. Two, he will obviously know I'm responsible if he comes home from work to find his place burgled or trashed. He might even think I did it myself out of spite. And I have seen first hand how he refuses to believe me when I tell him I didn't do something. And three, well, it's a damned nice neighborhood. It would be a waste of time. It's not the sort of place where an opportunist thief might see an open door and do their worst. Here, a neighbor is likely to see that the door has been left open and come and shut it for him.

I lock the door before I can change my mind and put the key through the letter box. Either he will find it, or he won't.

I don't care anymore. Except I do care. I do care and this is breaking my heart. But I know there's nothing I can do about it. I stated my case and Cullen chose not to believe me. I don't care how much this hurts, I refuse to resort to begging him to hear me out. I have not sunk that low yet.

I put my stuff in the trunk of my car and get in the driver's seat. I start the engine and pull away and head for home. I should probably start looking for another job, but I decide to give today over to moping around watching shitty daytime TV and being depressed. I will start the job hunt tomorrow.

Chapter 27

Max

I slam my apartment door and practically throw the suitcase and the bag of my stuff from the office onto the floor. I sit down and then I stand back up again. I go into the kitchen and pour myself a glass of water. I have a sip and put the glass back down. I don't know where I want to be or what I want to do. I have to stop this mindlessness though. It's not like Cullen was my whole life for fuck's sake. I managed to survive without him for all of those years before I met him and I'm sure I can learn to do it again.

So, what can I do instead of wandering around like I'm shell shocked?

I go back to the living room, and I sit down on the couch and turn the TV on. I flick aimlessly through the channels, not expecting much considering it is a weekday afternoon. I settle for a rerun of Friends. When is there ever not a rerun of Friends somewhere? I lay back and put my feet up. I need to let Harriet know what has happened and I get back up and go and get my purse. I get comfy again and dig my cellphone out of my purse. I would rather talk to Harriet, but I know I can't call her right now because I know she's at work so instead, I write a message out to her so she can read it when she finishes work. Once she does, I'm sure she will call me.

"I know you're at work and you can't talk so don't worry, I just need to get this out. Cullen and I broke up. Oh, and he fired me. I don't really know what the fuck happened, except someone did something and he thinks it was me and he didn't believe me when I said it wasn't me. I know that doesn't make a lot of sense out of context, but it will take too long to write it all out. I'll talk to you once you're done with work for tonight and fill you in properly."

I read back over my text message. I know she won't fully understand what I mean but I can't be bothered to change it and so I hit send. I put my cellphone down on the coffee table and try to concentrate on Friends. Luckily, I've seen it enough times to follow it without taking much notice because I can't make myself think about anything other than Cullen and the way he looked at me when he asked how I could betray him like that. He had been angry yes, but it was more than that. He looked completely broken.

Oh no, don't even go there, I think to myself. You are not going to get yourself to a place where you end up feeling sorry for him.

I swing my feet around and stand up abruptly. I grab the suitcase and the bag I dumped near the door, and I go through to my bedroom and unpack all of my things. I strip off my work clothes and hang them up too – after all I've hardly had them on for more than an hour or two. I go to the bathroom and get in the shower.

I make no effort to wash my hair or my body. I'm

already clean. I just stand under the spray and cry. I remember Cullen promising to never hurt me, and I know he meant physically, and he hasn't done that, but I really think a black eye would have hurt less than him thinking I was lying to him, especially with what it was about. He seriously thought I would do that just to get ahead in my career. I thought Cullen was my soulmate, that he knew me better than I knew myself almost. But for him to believe such terrible things about me, it means that in reality, he never really knew me at all and that hurts so much I don't know if I will ever truly recover from it.

I have to though. Or at least I have to stop crying. I'm not this person who mopes around and feels sorry for myself. But this feels different. It's not just that I've lost Cullen, but I've lost my job and my integrity too. And the worst thing about it all is that I didn't even fucking do anything wrong, and I don't know who did and why they wanted to blame me on it.

I've stood in the shower long enough that I have stopped crying and I get out and put a towel around my hair and put my robe on. I brush my teeth and then I towel dry my hair off and go to the bedroom. I lay on my bed for five minutes while my robe dries me off and then I get dressed in a pair of navy blue leggings and a yellow blouse. I comb my hair and return the robe to the bathroom. I go back out to the living room where the next episode of Friends is playing.

I sit down and I think for a moment, and I have a momentary brain wave. It lasts long enough that I pick my cellphone up, ready to call Cyber Safe and ask Bill Bryson what the hell he had had sent to him and what he had told Cullen. Even as I debate doing it, I know that there is no

point though. I know that deep down, and I put my cellphone back down before I can embarrass myself in front of
anyone else today. What can Bill tell me that Cullen didn't?
That someone emailed him in my name with information
only Cullen and I were meant to know. He obviously didn't
know who was really behind the email or he would have
told Cullen that instead of saying it was me.

That's another thing that kind of hurts. To know that
there is someone out there who hates me this much that
they would send this email and ruin my life. I didn't even
know I had any enemies, and I can't fathom out who the
hell it could be or why they would do it. Why would anyone
want to blow someone's world up like this? It just doesn't
make sense.

I must have dozed off on the couch because I wake up
with a jump. I don't know what time it is or how long I've
been asleep for. I check the time. I've only been asleep for
ten minutes or so. I don't know what woke me up with such
a jump; maybe I was having a nightmare or something.

A loud banging sound comes from my front door, and I
realize that must have been what woke me up. I'm momentarily confused. Who the hell can it be? Harriet won't have
finished work yet so even if she's read my text message it's
not her. And she won't have told anyone else; we never blab
the things we tell each other. I'm on nodding terms with my
neighbors, but we certainly don't visit each other so that
rules them out. My mom would expect me to be at work at
this time so it's not her.

A surge of excitement goes through me making the skin
on my lower back tingle with goosebumps. It has to be
Cullen come to apologize to me. I will hear him out, but I

am not going to make this too easy for him. He called me a liar and that's one thing I don't like at all. But I will forgive him eventually. Of course I will. How could I not?

The insistent knock on my door comes again, and I have to bite my lower lip to not be smiling when I get up and cross the room to the door. I pull it open, and my excitement is gone, replaced with a cold, hard knot of dread in my stomach. It's not Cullen standing there, but Ross, my ex-boyfriend, the last person on earth I would want to see.

I can't let him see that I'm still afraid of him. I need to stand up to him and get him to go away and leave me alone.

"What do you want?" I say.

Ross smiles and I get a glimpse of the charming man I originally met. It's hard to see Ross as anything but ugly now I have seen the true colors beneath his skin, but on the surface, he is a good-looking man and when he smiles, his face lights up in a way that makes him irresistible. Until you learn what he is capable of, there is no doubting the fact that he is attractive.

"Well, that wasn't quite the greeting I was hoping for from you, but never mind," Ross says. "I want to talk to you Max, that's all."

"No. I don't want to talk to you. I have nothing more to say to you," I reply.

Ross shrugs.

"That's ok. I'll talk. You just need to listen," he says.

I shake my head but before I can open my mouth to tell him no again, he speaks again and icy cold fingers of fear dance down my spine.

"I am not asking Max," he says. "I am going to talk to you, and you are going to listen to me. That's how it works.

It's called a conversation, and we are going to have one. We can do it the hard way, or we can do it the easy way, but either way, it's happening. Now are you going to be a lamb and let me in of your own accord, or do I need to make you move out of my way?"

The last thing I want is Ross in here, but I know that low, calm voice. It's the voice he uses when he is going to get his way no matter what, the voice that means if I step out of line, he will hurt me. I know I am not strong enough to fight him, and now he has decided he wants to come in, I can either stand aside and let him in, or I can stand here and get punched until I fall down, and he will come in any way, just stepping over me where I fall.

I step aside and try to smile, gesturing for Ross to come in.

"See, that wasn't so hard now was it," he says in a condescending tone that sets my teeth on edge as he comes inside and pushes the door closed behind him. It doesn't quite catch, but I leave it and follow Ross to the couch, not wanting to anger him further.

Chapter 28
Ross

Max is my girl. She has been since the moment I clapped eyes on her. And she was easy enough to woo back then. She agreed to go on a date with me, and then another and another, and before I knew it, she had agreed to be my girlfriend. As far as I'm concerned, that is for life. It's a commitment for all time not just for the good times. And I know Max herself will see that in time, she just needs me to show her the way, reel her in and show her that it's time for us to stop messing around and settle down together.

I know she's playing hard to get at the moment, but that's ok. I'm in this for the long haul, and I will play her games. I will fight for her, show her that I mean business and that she is mine and always will be.

I must admit that I was shocked when she left me out of the blue. We had been getting on so well, or at least I thought we had, and Max was really starting to learn what behavior was acceptable and what behavior wasn't to be repeated. I know that sometimes those lessons hurt her and

I hated having to be the one to lay down the law with her – it definitely hurt me more than it hurt her, and had to be strong to do it for her, put aside my own pain and remind myself that Max was worth every second of it. And she was. She is. She always will be worth the world.

When it hurt me so much to hurt her that I didn't think I could keep doing it, I always found a way because deep down, I knew it wasn't about me. It was for Max, for her own good and at some point in the future, I was confident that she would see that and thank me for it. But I don't need her to thank me for it. I wasn't doing it for thanks. I was doing it for her. For Max. Like I would do anything for her.

When Max first left me, I figured it was just a little lover's tiff type of thing we were having and that she would of course come back to me. She would say she was sorry and that she loved me, and I would of course forgive her, and she would never leave my side again. But she was playing harder than that. She really gave me the run around, screening my calls, blocking me on social media, pretending she wasn't home when I went around to her place. And just when I was starting to think the game was getting somewhat tedious, she massively upped the stakes and moved home and changed jobs.

I spent months looking for her. I started to get sick of it, but I knew it was part of the game and if I wanted to win my prize – my prize being Max of course – then I had to keep on playing the game. I knew what Max was doing. She wasn't really hiding from me; no, she was making sure I loved her enough, that I would look for her and not stop until I had found her.

Her friends were all in on it of course, pretending that

they didn't know where she had moved to or where she was working these days. No amount of charm could get them to talk. I debated resorting to threats, but it's not my job to teach every woman I encounter how to behave. It's only my job to teach these things to Max and maybe she wouldn't like it if I shared my knowledge with other women too.

I persevered, following her friends here, there, and everywhere, and eventually, dearest Harriet led me to Max's apartment building. Of course I didn't know for sure it was hers at first, but even the first time I followed Harriet there, I got a little tingle of recognition in my veins, and I just knew somehow that this was the place. It was a new place for Harriet to visit which made me suspect it was Max's new place, and I staked the place out for a few days.

Of course, I had been wrong before and wasted many days staking out places that Harriet or one of Max's other girlfriends visited that seemed out of their normal routines, only for it to be a new boyfriend's place or a different friend had moved. This time though, I wasn't wrong, and it wasn't time wasted. I didn't realize quite how much I had missed her until I saw Max leave the building one day and I knew then that all of the searching and dead ends and time spent had been worth it.

I felt like it was still too early in the game yet for me to try and win her back. I didn't know anything about this new life of hers and I needed to know everything to prove to her that she was my life, my everything. So, I watched the building for a bit longer, and the next time Harriet visited, I watched her from the street. She got into the elevator and the red number one lit up above it and then the red number two and it stopped. That gave me Max's floor number and the next part was easy.

I rang each bell in turn and if a voice I didn't recognize answered, I said sorry wrong apartment, but when Max answered, I just hung up, and then I had her apartment number. By then, I had staked the place out enough to see that the main door of the apartment complex didn't lock. Residents and regular visitors alike just walked in without a key or pausing to ring a bell. That convinced me this was the right thing to do. It was like a sign from the universe confirming to me that I was on the right path.

Once I had Max's full address, the rest just fell into place. With little more than Google, I was able to find Max's cellphone provider and from there, her new number. But I didn't call her. Instead, I called a friend of mine, a hacker I had met years before, and became good friends with. I convinced him to hack into Max's cellphone for me so that I could learn what I needed to know before I made my move.

Once the hack was completed, I wasn't able to listen in on Max's calls, but I got a copy of every text message, DM and email she sent, plus a recording of any voicemails she left or received. That was how I found out about her starting to see Cullen.

I must admit that hurt me badly. There is a difference between playing hard to get and wanting me to prove my love, and outright cheating on me. That's a lesson I'm going to have to teach Max.

I mean what did this dude have that I didn't? Ok, from following him and researching him and his company, I soon found out the answers to that. A billion dollar company, a better car than I could ever hope to drive, everything a woman seemed to want basically. But come on, the guy's name is Cullen for fuck's sake. Who calls a baby that?

Anyway, I pushed my jealousy aside and learned about Max's new job, and her new life without me. I knew that I couldn't wait forever to make my move, but as time went on, I will admit that I held myself back from making a move because I got scared that she might actually choose Cullen over me. Obviously, I wouldn't allow that to actually happen – she is mine, not his - but it would hurt none the less knowing that would have been her choice if I was willing to give her one. I started obsessing over what to do, what to say, and I just kept watching, waiting for the right moment.

Just when I was about convinced the right moment would never come and I either needed to make a move or give up and stop wasting my time on Max, the universe came through for me again and showed me another sign.

I knew my first move had to be to get Cullen out of the picture, and when I saw the email Max sent to herself from her cellphone with an audio recording of some sort of pitch to a new client on it, I knew exactly what to do. And it worked.

It didn't work in the way I thought it would. I figured the guy I sent the information to would use it to under cut Cullen's firm and then once that was done, I would have to find a way to let him know Max was the one who sabotaged him – or at least that's how it would look. But it worked out so much better than that. Within hours of me sending the email, Max was texting Harriet saying her and Cullen were over, and that she had been fired too. The next part of her message didn't make much sense, but it sounded like the man I emailed pretending to be Max had enough morals to contact Cullen instead of using the information and Max lost everything in one fell swoop. I knew then that it was time to make my move and show Max that she didn't need Cullen or his stupid job. All she needed was me.

When her life was falling apart, I would swoop in like her knight in shining armor and make everything ok again.

As soon as I read and deciphered that text message, I instantly made my way over to her apartment building. I'm here now, inside of her apartment and I'm going to make her see that I am the only man for her. I won't fuck this up. I have to get my Max back. And I will do whatever it takes to make sure that happens.

Chapter 29
Max

Ross sits at one end of the couch, and I take the other end, doing my best to keep as much distance as possible between us without making it obvious I'm doing so. I must succeed in doing it subtly because if Ross thought I was doing it on purpose, he would have something to say about it no doubt. That's why I took the other end of the couch instead of one of the arm chairs. It's just easier to do things his way when it's something as small as where I should sit.

I can see my cellphone on the coffee table out of the corner of my eye and part of me wants to make a grab for it, but Ross will just take it away from me. And even if I manage to get it without him seeing, what then? Who am I going to call?

I could call my mom, but there's no way I would risk bringing her into this. I could call Harriet, but she'll still be at work and probably wouldn't even be able to pick up, let alone come to my rescue. I could call the police and tell them I willingly let this man into my apartment, and now he is sitting here not touching or harming me, but I need their help. Yes, I know how that one would go down. None of my friends know how bad things were with Ross and me except for Harriet, so calling any of them wouldn't work; they would think I was just being dramatic. Which leaves Cullen. It always comes back to Cullen.

I'm not sure he would even care that Ross is here and that I am terrified of him, but even if he had enough affection left for me to care enough to get Ross out of here for me, the stubborn streak in me doesn't want to go to him for help. Not after everything that has happened between us. I don't want him to know that I still need him, and I certainly don't want him to know how few options I have if I need someone's help.

"Aren't you going to offer me a drink?" Ross says, smirking at me.

"Would ... would you like a cup of coffee or something?" I say.

I know when to pick my battles and this one isn't it. If he wants a drink, he can have a drink.

"No thank you, but it's good to be asked. It's always nice to be nice Max," he says.

"I agree," I say, forcing myself to smile at him. "I wasn't trying to be rude. I thought you wanted to talk to me, and I figured that was more important than serving refreshments."

It seems I have said the wrong thing, because Ross slams a fist down into the arm of my couch. I try not to let him see me flinch, but he probably does. He doesn't comment on it, but that doesn't mean he hasn't noticed and is storing it up to use against me somehow later. That's his style.

"See that's what happens when you try to second guess me Max. Stop doing that ok. Just do what I tell you to do and then I won't have to keep hurting you. Why don't you understand that?" Ross says.

How didn't I see this layer of crazy in him before? He's speaking as though he is genuinely the long suffering victim here, and I'm some sort of project to be worked on and molded, a task forced on him whether he wants it or not, but because he is so heroic and good, he will strive to take it all on and complete the task and help me to become a model citizen or whatever shit it is he thinks he's doing.

"Has it ever occurred to you that I might not want to do whatever it is you are telling me I have to do?" I say.

I cringe inside at my mouth for running away with my thoughts before I could sensor them. I wait for Ross to blow up, but instead, he just smiles and shakes his head.

"I know I lose my temper sometimes, but I don't mean to honey. I know it's not your fault. If that mother of yours had taught you better, you would be better," he says.

"Don't you dare bring my mom into this," I snap, my anger at him implying my mom somehow failed me momentarily overcoming my fear of making Ross angry.

"Oh, I've touched a nerve there, have I?" Ross says and laughs. His laughter fades and he shakes his head. "No actually you're right. I like Hayley. And I do believe she did her best. If anyone is to blame, it's your so called father. He should have been around disciplining you, showing you what it takes to please a man."

I don't reply to that because I have no words. At least not ones that won't end up with me getting a fist in my face, something I would prefer to avoid if I can. And I owe my deadbeat dad nothing, so I don't feel like I need to defend him.

"I wanted to express my condolences actually," Ross says after a moment of silence. "I'm sorry to hear that you lost your job and your boyfriend."

He spits out the word boyfriend like it burns his mouth, but I ignore that for now. I'm more taken aback by the fact that he knows this. How can he possibly know it? Even if he was following me, and saw me crying in the car, he wouldn't know why. Even if he took a guess, he might be lucky and guess I had been fired or dumped, but both? Nah. I'm not buying it.

I'm almost certain Sam must have caved and gave him my address because I know Harriet wouldn't, but she can't have told him about this because she doesn't even know herself yet. And even if Harriet had stabbed me in the back, which I know she wouldn't, she wouldn't have had time to receive my text, read it, and contact Ross in time for him to get over here when he did. None of it makes sense.

"How do you know about that?" I ask.

"The words you are looking for Max honey is, thank you for your condolences," Ross says.

Here we go. Even before he showed me his violent side, he had this pompous side where he thinks everyone should have the manners of a really formal setting at all times.

"Thank you for your condolences," I say. "But how did you know to offer them?"

My wording must meet his standards this time because he doesn't make an effort to correct me. He doesn't answer my question either. He just winks and taps the side of his nose. Maybe I should tell him that it is rude to answer a question with a gesture and it is also rude to withhold information you have been asked about. But I know better than to start an argument with him.

Well actually, no, that's not true. I'm going to end up arguing with him to get him to leave, I know that much. But I know how to pick my battles and I am not going to get into an argument with him this early on or by the time I try to get him to leave, he will have riled himself up into the kind of temper that scares me; I'm certain that if I had stayed with him, that temper would have caused him to kill me one day. And to be honest, I don't care if he has manners or not.

I am curious if my guess at Sam spilling my address is true though and while I'm asking questions and not getting yelled at for it, I decide to ask one more. I don't really expect an answer other than another nose tap, but I decide to ask anyway.

"How did you find me here?" I ask.

"Oh, it was easier than you might think," he says. "I just followed your bestie around for long enough that eventually, she came here."

Sorry Sam I say inside my head. It shows how easy it is for someone determined to find me to do it without anyone even knowing about it. It's kind of a scary thought, but I don't have time to worry about that now. I have enough of a scary situation to deal with as it is without starting to think about others.

"I can't say I was happy about the Cullen development," Ross says. He says Cullen in the same hissing tone he said boyfriend earlier. "But don't worry. I'm not mad. Well maybe I am a little bit, but I get it. I understand what you were trying to do, that you wanted to make me jealous.

Well honey, it sure worked but I will forgive you for seeing him behind my back, because I know that now you have my attention, you won't do it again."

I don't even know where to begin to process that. He really is more deranged than I have ever known him to be, to the point where it's actually scarier than him yelling the odds at me.

"I didn't do anything behind your back," I say. "We weren't together when Cullen and I got together."

"Ah so sweet that you are trying to save my feelings, but there's really no need to. Like I said, I have already forgiven you," Ross says. "But please don't imply that there was ever a time we weren't together in spirit even if not in physical proximity."

"No," I say. "We didn't have some sort of long distance romance. We split up, Ross."

"Shh now," he says, his voice gentle like he is soothing a baby. "Let it go Max. None of that matters now, I'm here with you and this time I am not letting you go again."

That is a horrible thought, but I still can't quite get past the fact that he thinks we have been together this whole time. Like what? How does he even come up with this stuff?

"Ross, please. Be rational here. We haven't spoken in well over eight months. How can you possibly think we are still together," I say.

"Ok, ok, we'll play it your way. You always did like to get your own way," Ross says giving me an indulgent smile, like he's doing me a favor. I suppose in his mind he is. God what a condescending prick he is. How did I ever find this man attractive? "We broke up."

He puts broke up in inverted commas, telling me he still isn't taking this seriously.

"I don't even know what to say at this point," I say and that is completely honest.

"You don't have to say anything honey. I know you needed that time to figure things out and that's good that you have been able to do so. Don't get me wrong, I missed you, but we have our whole lives ahead of us now and we get to spend them together without you always wondering if you made a mistake because you know for sure now that you didn't. The universe brought us back to each other."

"No, you stalked my friends, got my address, and forced your way in here. That's not the universe telling us to do anything," I say.

If I had taken a moment to think it through, I wouldn't have dared say that to him, but as it is, it's said now and there's nothing I can do to take it back.

"You never were a romantic," Ross muses.

Chapter 30

Max

He says it with an indulging smile, like we are a new couple out on a date, and he is pointing something out about me in a cute, teasing kind of a way. There is nothing cute or teasing about it in the scenario we are in though. It's horrifying how utterly delusional he is, and I don't know how to handle this. It seems that whatever I say, he is going to just gloss over it and make it fit this fantasy he has built up in his head.

I know if I anger him or try anything like running from him now, he is likely to flip out completely and hurt me. As much as I hate the idea of even pretending that I feel anything for him, I'm starting to think that my only way out of this might be to go along with him and then when he leaves it's not me kicking him out but him going home in his mind. I can then hopefully get away from here and get some help before his next visit.

The thing is though, that might work short-term, but to really throw him off my scent it will mean uprooting my whole life again, moving into a new place. And I don't want to keep running.

I'm thinking of the big picture and it's too big to consider with Ross sitting beside me in my apartment. I need to concentrate on one thing at a time, and right now, my priority is simply getting Ross out of my apartment in the here and now without me being hurt. That's it. That's all I have to focus on right now.

"I guess not," I say with what I hope is a convincing self-conscious shrug.

"Oh, honey it's ok. I love you just as you are," Ross says.

My shrug must have been convincing. Maybe I can pull this off. Maybe Cullen was right but for reasons he doesn't even know about, and I should start looking for work as an actress. Ross is looking at me and I can't read his expression which is worrying me.

"You can say it back you know," he says quietly after a moment. He looks at me with piercing eyes and I realize he's waiting for me to tell him that I love him.

I try to say it, I really do, but the words just won't come out.

"Max," Ross says, his voice starting to sound less amused and more angry. "Tell me that you love me."

"I ... I can't. It's too soon," I say.

Surely that's better than saying I can't because I fucking hate you.

"How can it be too soon? We've been together for months now Max," Ross says.

"No, we haven't," I yell. I didn't want to lose my patience, but I can't help it. There's only so much of his delusion I can play along with before it drives me insane.

"We dated and we broke up. This might be eight months in for you, but for me, it's day one."

It's the best I can do to also continue to try to play along by letting him think I'm still open to some sort of reconciliation with him. I hope it's going to be enough, but his expression tells me it isn't going to be. I seem to remember that being a thing with Ross. It didn't matter how much I gave him, he always wanted more.

He jumps up off the sofa, and I flinch, but he doesn't come towards me, he just starts pacing up and down in front of the coffee table.

"I really thought we were getting somewhere Max. I thought we were going to be able to put all of this mess behind us finally, but no. You won't do anything the easy way will you? God Max, why do you always make me punish you? Do you think I like having to teach you this stuff? Because I don't. It hurts me deep inside," he says.

"So don't do it then," I counter.

"I have to do it. I can put up with the pain for you, my love. Because someone has to teach you. I'm sorry for getting angry there. I know you're doing your best. Maybe I'm just not the best teacher. But we'll get there won't we? Even if the progress is pretty slow. Because love conquers everything," Ross says.

The really scary thing about all of this is that I genuinely think Ross believes everything he's saying here. He believes that we are in love and that I just need help to be a better person, and by help, he means a beating to keep me in line. And he sees nothing wrong with this because he actually does believe it's for my sake not his, that he's really helping me.

I need to try a different tactic because I can't tell this man I love him. I don't think I would ever be able to get him to leave my side if I do but telling him that it is too soon isn't working. That's just going to result in him hurting me – for my own good of course.

Come on Max. Think. There has to be something you can say to make him believe you. An idea occurs to me, and I look down into my lap, hoping I look ashamed of myself.

"I … I'm sorry. You're right of course. Love is enough and I'm sorry I can't say it yet, but I lied about why," I start.

This gets Ross's attention, and I can feel his eyes on me as he waits for me to explain what I mean. I think about how I feel about Cullen and how, despite everything, when we were together, I still hadn't been brave enough to tell him that I loved him.

"It's such a big, loaded word and I feel like our relationship is still kind of new. I'm scared that it changes things between us," I say. I force myself to look up at him and smile. "I guess I'm scared I'll come on too strong and scare you away."

Ross comes towards me, but I don't think he's going to hurt me. He's smiling and it's not his arrogant smirk. He perches on the coffee table opposite me and gently strokes my cheek. It takes everything I have not to cringe away from his touch, but I manage it.

"You never, ever have to worry about that with me honey," he says. "You could never scare me away. Now say it. Tell me that you love me. I need to hear it."

I just shake my head. I can't do it. Even if it means him hitting me, I will take it because I can't sully those words by saying them to him.

"It's ok, I get it," Ross says, and his voice is still gentle and soothing, like he really does get it. "They say actions speak louder than words anyway don't they. So don't tell me that you love me. Show me that you love me."

He doesn't give me a chance to refuse him. He leans in and tries to kiss me. I pull back just seconds before his lips touch mine and he pulls back too, the soft look on his face melting away to anger once more.

"Oh, so it's like that is it? You're too good to even kiss me now, are you?" he snarls.

I don't respond because I know anything I say at this point will only anger him further. He jumps up from the coffee table.

"Well? What do you have to say for yourself bitch? No clever excuses this time? Do you think I'm stupid Max? Do you think you can just tell me any old crap and I will believe it? Well, you can't, and I won't," he shouts.

Maybe if he shouts loud enough for long enough, one of my neighbors will call the police. I doubt it though. As far as I know, the other people close enough to hear anything from my apartment all work so they likely won't be home in the middle of the afternoon on a week day. And even if they are home, they probably won't call the police for a bit of shouting. I wouldn't if I heard my neighbors having a row, and to anyone who doesn't know the dynamic between me and Ross, that's all this would sound like at this point.

He raises his hand, his palm open and swipes towards my face like he is about to slap me. I hate that I cringe away, showing my fear. I didn't want him to know how scared I am, but I can't help it. It's a natural reaction when you're about to get hit by someone bigger and stronger than you are.

The hit doesn't come. Instead, Ross grabs a handful of my hair. I squeal as he pulls me to my feet by it.

"Shut up," he snarls. "Stop fucking squealing."

"You're ... you're hurting me," I say somewhat pointlessly, I guess. He must know he's hurting me – he's pulling me about by my hair for fuck's sake. He knows.

"No Max. Your actions are hurting you. I'm just showing you what happens when you defy me," Ross says.

Several smart ass remarks run through my head, but I manage to keep them in. Now really isn't the time to rile him up further than he already is. He still has a fistful of my hair in his hand, and although he isn't actively pulling it now, if I set him off, I know from experience that he won't hesitate to rip it out of my scalp.

He looks at me for a moment and then he nods to himself like he has come up with some sort of a plan. I don't know what it is and to be honest, I don't want to know what it is, because the one thing I do know is that whatever it is, it won't be pleasant for me.

"I think you have forgotten how good we were together," he says.

He releases my hair from his fist, and I feel a moment of relief. It doesn't last long though because his hand caresses my cheek again and I have to make a conscious effort not to recoil away from his touch.

"Let me kiss you and you will remember. Don't fight me on this Max," he says.

Chapter 31

Max

He leans in to kiss me, but of course I do fight him in the only way that I can. I pull my head backwards as he moves his forwards. He sighs like me not wanting him to violate me is annoying him. Boo fucking hoo.

"I've tried to do this the easy way Max. I have been gentle and understanding and I have tried to ease you back into being with me, but you have thrown it back in my face at every turn. Please remember that," Ross says.

He looks at me for a moment longer and I don't know what he's waiting for or what he wants me to say to that. I have no words that will help my cause right now, so I just stand there looking back at him. Despite that, he still takes me by surprise when he bursts into movement. He grabs me by my shoulders and forces me past the end of the couch and then he slams me against the nearest wall. I cry out and he puts his hand over my mouth.

I try to kick him, but he brings his feet down on mine, one on each, holding them in place. I punch at him with my

179

fists on his back and arms and chest, but he is so much bigger than me and so much stronger than me that my touches probably feel like nothing more than a minor annoyance to him.

He lets me attack him for a few minutes longer and then he grabs my wrists. He pushes my hands above my head against the wall and puts them together so that he can grip both of my wrists in one of his much bigger hands. It's only when his other hand starts back towards my mouth that I realize I was free to yell again for a moment there, and I missed my chance. I was in too much of a horrified state from losing both my hands and my feet as weapons.

He puts his hand back over my mouth and I make an "mm" sound as I try to get away, my nostrils flaring as I breath frantically through them. I try to get my hands free and then I try to get my feet free, but nothing is working. and Ross isn't even building up a sweat restraining me. He is just watching me with the expression a child might wear whilst watching a fly stuck in a spider's web. And my thrashing against Ross has about as much of an effect on him as a fly trying to free itself from the sticky web would have on the spider.

I need a new tactic, something to force him to release me. I still don't know what I will do if he does release me, but I remind myself that I'm working in baby steps here – one at a time and no more - and I need him to get off me. I can't stand the feeling of his skin against mine, the closeness of his body to me.

An idea comes to me, and I do it before I can change my mind and wuss out. I quickly bite down on the palm of Ross's hand. I know I will only get one chance at this and so

I make it a good one, biting down hard enough to make him cry out. And I don't let go when he tries to pull his hand away. Instead, I dig my teeth in harder and shake my head from side to side like a starving dog killing its prey.

But this is like a role reversal because sharp teeth or not, I'm still the prey and Ross is very much the predator. I sense rather than see movement at my side and a second later, I hear the clapping sound of flesh against flesh. I feel a stinging pain in my cheek so intense that it makes my skin feel wet. Instinctively, I open my mouth to cry out and this releases Ross's palm from my grip between my teeth as my head flies to the side.

The pain in my face is so intense and I can feel heat flaring up where I've been hit too. If I could see myself in a mirror right now, I know I would be able to see a red and inflamed hand print on my face. I go to bring my hand to my cheek, to press it against the pain, but Ross still has both of my wrists in his one hand, and he isn't letting go of me.

"You just had to, didn't you? You had to spoil our reunion and make me hurt you," he says. "I don't know what sort of people you have had in your life since you walked away from me, but they have turned you into some sort of filthy animal. You ... you bit me Max. That's what animals do, not ladies."

He sounds so surprised when he says that I bit him, and he brings his palm up in front of his face to have a look at it. In other circumstances, the shocked expression on his face, his open-jawed mouth, and wide eyes, would actually be funny, but I'm really not in the mood to laugh right now. Not even close to it.

"I'm done being nice now. I am going to kiss you. You

will kiss me back and then you will tell me that you love me. Or I will make you do it," Ross says.

I have no doubt that he can and will make me bend to his will and say that I love him. I am going to hold out for as long as I can though, and even if he beats me senseless and makes me say it to stop the pain, we will both know that I don't mean it, that I'm just saying it to save myself from a beating.

I have spent most of this encounter trying my best to placate Ross and keep him calm and that has gotten me nowhere and I feel a spark of anger and rebellion bloom inside of me, and I decide that if this bastard is going to hurt me, I am going to hurt him first. Maybe not physically. Even the bite I gave him did little more than make his skin red and piss him off. But mentally and emotionally, I know how to cut him to the bone, and I give him a small smile that he must take for agreement, because he smiles back at me encouragingly.

"Say it Max," he whispers.

"I will never say those words to you Ross. Not because it's too soon, or because I am afraid that I will scare you away. I won't say those words to you because they are simply not true. I don't love you. I love Cullen," I say.

I can see that my shot hit home. I see the pain in Ross's eyes, and for a moment, I feel a stab of pain too, because telling him I love Cullen reminds me that I have lost Cullen. And I didn't even tell him how I truly felt about him. But now isn't the time to go down that tangent.

"You had better keep that name out of your damned mouth girl because you and him are done. You are with me now and nothing and no one will keep us apart this time," he says.

He leans down to kiss me, and I turn my head to the side. His lips rub against my cheek and even that sends a shiver of revulsion through me, but it's better than him getting to put his lips on mine.

"Don't fucking test me here Max," he says, and he grabs my face in his spare hand. He comes in from beneath my jaw, his hand angled so that I am half choked, and he squeezes my cheeks hard enough to hurt me, and also hard enough to make my lips pop out in a parody of someone puckering up their lips for a kiss.

When he comes in to try and kiss me again, I try to turn my head away, but I can't do it. He holds me in place, and I can feel his hot breath on my lips, and I know it's only a second until his lips touch mine. I squeeze my eyes closed because I can't bear to see his face so close to mine, and tears spring from my eyes and slowly run down my face as I wait for the moment something breaks inside of me.

Chapter 32
Cullen

The moment I see the email from Bill Bryson with the attachment of Max's email and her notes from the meeting we had with Mr McPherson, I feel like something inside of me has died. I can feel myself hyper-ventilating, the pain shooting through my chest and stomach. She has betrayed me. The one woman I really thought I loved and who loved me in return has been acting this whole time. I take a moment to concentrate on slowing my breathing and as I do it, the pains across my torso and abdomen ease off. I am still shaken to the core though and although the breathing exercises calm me enough that my body doesn't react in such an intense way, emotionally, I am still a wreck.

When Bill had first called me and told me he had received an email from a member of my staff stabbing me in the back I didn't believe him. Especially when he said that the name of that member of my staff was Max, the last person at the company I would think would want stab me in the back. But he told me that he had proof and that he would send it to me. And now he has, and he has ruined everything. I want to just pretend none of this has happened, but as nice as it would be to just not have to deal with this, I know I have to because whether I like it or not, I can't unsee what I saw.

I try to tell myself that while Bill wasn't lying about the email, that it isn't necessarily true that everything between me and Max is a lie, that maybe I'm missing something. I'm pretty sure I'm not missing anything, but I keep holding onto the hope that I am, that she will have some sort of explanation for the email, something that will make it ok. Something that we will both end up laughing about in the years to come. Or even something that doesn't quite make sense that I can choose to believe will do.

I can't think of anything that it could be that could explain everything without it ending in me being betrayed, but I have to have hope. And I force myself to hold onto that tiny shred of it and I hope against hope that she has something, anything that I can cling onto so that I can convince myself that I haven't been duped by her after all, and that everything that we have is real.

I need to stop thinking and do something physical to try and distract my brain. I get up and I pace up and down my office, back and forth, back and forth. I do this for about fifteen minutes, but it doesn't really do anything for me except make me feel dizzy. I stop pacing and leave my office. I go to the breakroom because people in the company will think I'm crazy if they see me just pacing around the corridors and I am not ready to go back to my office yet because I feel like I still can't think straight. I grab a coffee and drink it standing up in the breakroom. The caffeine seems to help me feel a bit better and I head back to my office. For all I know I will still have the same problems when I go back there, the last thing I want is someone coming into the breakroom and trying to talk to me. Even though I feel better than I did five minutes ago, I'm hardly in the mood to pass the time of day with someone. I need to think, but clearly and logically, not chat.

I keep wondering when Max was planning to leave, both her role at the company and her role as my girlfriend, and for a few minutes. I wonder briefly if I should try to beat her at her own game and not let on that I know she has been playing a game here with me. I could see then what exactly her end goal is. Although I guess that her end goal is pretty obvious. She must have figured that she could use the information to leverage herself a deal at Cyber Safe. But what she hadn't counted on was Bill being a moral sort who wouldn't act on something like what she had sent him, and she definitely wouldn't have counted on him giving me the head's up about one of my staff sabotaging me like this. She probably saw herself going to Cyber Safe in the next few days, announcing who she was, and being offered a position and a huge corner office on the spot.

Whatever end game Max has and whatever game she is playing, I decide I'm not going to stoop to that level, and I'm not going to hide from this. I am self-aware enough to know that telling myself I want to see how far she will go with it is just a way out for me, a way to put off the inevitable and it has gone way past that now. I'm going to have to confront her. It's the only thing I can do. And the longer I leave it, the harder it will get to bring it up, and at some point, she will leave, and I will be as blindsided as I was this morning, only this time, I will have no one to blame for that but myself.

I'm still clinging on to that tiny little ray of hope I have left that there will somehow be a reasonable explanation for it all, but if there isn't, then at least I will have the satisfaction of letting Max know that I knew all about her little act before she was ready to spring the truth on me, and that she was no longer going to be able to play me like her favorite tune on an old guitar. It was a small victory, but it was a victory all the same and if I lost everything else, I would take what tiny victories I could get.

With the decision made, I scrawl a note for Max: 'Come to my office immediately when you get in'.

It is cold and to the point, but it is also impersonal enough that if another member of staff happens to see it, it doesn't give anything personal away. I don't want this being the next bout of office gossip no matter what the outcome is. I take the note and put it on Max's desk where she can't miss it, and then I go back to my office.

I keep thinking of this morning, how Max and I were together and how we even came together. Surely, she can't have been faking that the whole time we were fucking. I know she wasn't. She could make all the right noises and pull all off the right faces, but no one is a good enough actress to gush the way she does when she comes. So yes, she probably did genuinely enjoy the sex if nothing else.

And after we had sex, I told her to have a half day off because she was doing a good job and the whole time, she was double crossing me. God, I am such a frigging idiot. I might as well have just bent over in front of her and said, here have at it, take every shred of my dignity.

She must think I'm so fucking stupid, so blind to not see what she was doing right under my nose. I suppose she's not wrong. I was blinded by the way she made me feel and for once, I listened to my heart instead of my head. That was a big mistake as I always feared it would be. I will learn from it though and I won't make that same mistake again, not with her and not with anyone else either.

I look at the clock and nine minutes have passed since I last looked at it and it feels like at least an hour or two has passed by. I guess it's going to be a long morning waiting for her to get into the office so that we can hash this thing out but there's really nothing I can do except wait now. I could call her and tell her to get her ass in here, but that might give her the head's up that I'm onto her and give her time to come up with some sort of story. I don't that. I want to get her actual reaction when I confront her with this, and I want to be able to see her face and her body language, not just hear her voice. It is much harder to do the right expressions and display the right body language than it is to just lie with words. She's obviously good at it, or I would have seen it before now, but now that I know what I'm looking for, where before, I had no reason to doubt her, so I wasn't looking for the signs of lies.

By the time I'm expecting Max to be showing up, some of the pain I had felt at first has given way to anger which I think will help me confront her in a logical way rather than in an emotional way.

I keep thinking about how I had helped this girl when she needed help. How I had taken a chance on a stranger and given her a job and how I had overlooked the fact that she made mistakes on important things at first. And then I had given her my heart and she had crumpled it up like scrap paper and thrown it away. How could she do that to me? And how could she still look me in the eye knowing what she had done? How had she let me fuck her this morning before work knowing it was all an act and that the game was going to be up soon enough?

I didn't much like feeling angry like this, but it was better than the broken feeling I had experienced earlier. Especially when it came to be time to confront Max. I feel like I'm more in control of my emotions now which means I'm less likely to break down in front of Max or to believe any more bullshit just because I so desperately want to believe in her, in us.

A light tap at my office door comes as I sit staring at the invoice I'm meant to be checking over and approving. I have had it open for over half an hour now and it's literally a two minute job, I just can't focus on it.

That tap on my door tells me that Max is here, and I'm both relieved that we are about to get this over with and nervous that it will go badly. But at least once it's done, I might be able to concentrate enough to complete simple tasks again. I take a deep, steadying breath and I force my face into a neutral expression, something I learned to do for meeting with clients when I needed them not to know what I was thinking.

"Come in," I call, and I'm pleased that my voice sounds level and normal, as neutral as my facial expression. I well and truly have my game face on now.

Chapter 33
Cullen

My office door opens and Max steps into the room. She is wearing a black pencil skirt with a pale pink blouse, and I hate that the sight of her still takes my breath away, even now. The skirt skims over her hips, showing off those gorgeous curves.

Stop it, I think to myself. You are not going to get through this if you spend the whole time thinking about how hot Max is.

She closes the door behind her and stays standing by the it like she is awaiting some sort of instruction. Her face is slightly flushed, and she is watching me, seemingly waiting for me to smile or wink or to give her some indication that I want her. I won't let her get the upper hand though. Not this time. She's had more than her fair share of having that and now it's my turn.

"Take a seat," I snap.

Max heads toward the chair opposite mine, but at the last minute, she diverts herself and comes around behind my desk. What the fuck is she playing at? Before I can really work out what's happening, she is behind me and she wraps her arms around my shoulders from behind, something that even now makes my cock come to life in anticipation of what is to come.

"Have I been a bad girl?" Max says playfully into my ear, her breath tickling my skin and making it tingle.

I ache for her, and I know I have to get her off me if I am going to be able to do this. If I can't even stop her touching me, I have no chance of getting the truth out of her. I need her to know that I mean business here. With that in mind, I reach up and take one of Max's hands in each of mine and pull them off my shoulders. She doesn't resist me, but I hear her swallow loudly and I know she wasn't expecting that reaction from me, and she is in uncertain territory now. Good, because that makes two of us.

"This is serious Max," I say, using my cold and emotionless 'CEO voice'. "Sit down please."

Max surprises me a little bit by doing what I say. She goes and sits down in the chair opposite mine, but she doesn't look sheepish or ashamed of her actions. She sits there, as bold as brass, looking me dead in the eye and it sends another surge of anger through me. It hasn't even occurred to her that I might be onto her.

"I don't ..." I start, ready to tell Max that I don't want to hear her bullshit anymore and to get out of my sight. But the truth is, angry or not, I am still clinging to the hope that she can explain this. I tell myself that it's only fair that I give her that chance and that's why I'm doing this, not because I so badly want to be wrong here. I stop myself from saying what I planned to say, but I can't seem to stop myself from talking until I think of something better, and instead, a more heartfelt statement comes out of my mouth. "How could you betray me like that?" It's not what I wanted to say, but it really is the question whose answer lies right at the heart of this matter.

I watch her, looking for sign of discomfort, but there's no sign of her fiddling with her fingers, or picking at her clothes. She's not even shuffling in her chair. Oh, she's good. She is really fucking good, like another level good. She is looking at me like she has absolutely no idea what I'm talking about, and I don't know whether I want to congratulate her on a great performance or shake her and scream in her face for lying to me. I do neither obviously. Instead, I wait to see what she is going to say.

"I don't know what you mean," she says finally, and it sounds so truthful that I almost apologize for doubting her and send her on her way. I can't do that though. She knows what she's done and either she can explain it in a way I can live with, or she can't; it's that simple.

"You can drop the innocent act Max," I say.

I'm done playing around, nibbling at the edges of the issue. It's time to get everything out in the open.

"It isn't an act," Max says. She is looking at me like I've lost my mind and for a moment, I wonder if I have, but then I remember Bill's email and I know I haven't. "I genuinely have no idea what you're talking about. I haven't betrayed you in any way."

So, she's going to play it this way then. I kind of hoped she would make it easy, but I should have known better than that. Even on her best days, nothing is ever easy or straight forward with Max. It made being with her challenging in a good way and I liked that about her, but right now, it is just pissing me off. There's challenging and then there's this shit.

"Are you really going to make me spell it out for you?" I ask, giving her a final chance to just admit to what she's done and get this over with.

"I guess so because unless you do, I will still have no idea what we're talking about here," Max replies.

So, this is how she's going to play it then. She is going to stick to her story like a safety blanket until I pull it out from underneath her altogether then. I suppose there's a chance she only thinks I suspect something rather than have proof of it, and that if she can lie well enough, I will believe her when she insists that she has done nothing wrong. She obviously doesn't know that Bill has emailed me so she thinks she can convince me that I have it all wrong. It's time to drop that card in her lap and see what she does with it.

"Does the name Bill Bryson mean anything to you?" I ask.

Max pauses for a moment like she's thinking. She's really good at this. She should be a spy or some shit. She shakes her head after a moment.

"No," she says.

"What about Cyber Safe?" I ask. "Have you heard of them?"

If she says no again, then I will know she's lying. Everyone in the industry has heard of Cyber Safe, just like everyone in the industry has heard of ITSafe, too. Max must know that I know this, and she doesn't try to deny it. She nods her head.

"Now we're getting somewhere," I say. I want to know

how much information she is willing to give up at this point. "Who are they?"

"One of the firm's competitors," she says.

I'm pretty sure that's the first true thing she has said since telling me she has been a bad girl.

"Correct," I say icily and then I elaborate slightly. "In fact, they are the company's biggest competitor, and the McPherson Financial Solutions contract was going to ensure that we stayed heads and shoulders above them. And it still will, no thanks to you."

I expect my final line to get some sort of a reaction. A denial or the startled look of a rabbit caught in headlights, but no. She has the fucking audacity to look at me like I have the lost the plot. I am not going to fall for her shit. She knows exactly what I'm talking about, and I know she does, and what makes it even worse is that at this point, she knows I know that she knows. But maybe she still doesn't know for sure how much I know, only that I know something. It's time to lay my next card in her lap.

"Ok, I get it. You want to know how much I know so that you know how much to admit to. Well, I know all of it, but I'll play along," I tell her. "Bill Bryson is the head of new customer acquisitions at Cyber Safe. Do you know what his job is?"

"No, because I don't know him," Max says. She stops there and I wait, an old police trick to keep a suspect talking by leaving an uncomfortable silence they feel the need to fill. It works, but what Max says next doesn't give much away. "But if I had to guess, going off the job title, I would say he is in charge of getting new clients for his firm."

"Ring a ding ding," I say sarcastically. She looks like

she's about to say something else, but she had her chance to talk and it's my turn now and I don't let her interrupt me. "Imagine my horror when I get a call today from Bill Bryson. Because we might be rivals, but Bill is like me – old school, and he likes to play fair. He told me that he got an email from you with the full proposal I put forward for Mr McPherson. Care to explain that?"

She blinks at me a couple of times like she is shocked I have said that, but I think she is using this time to come up with a response. I wait. I have all of the time in the world for this.

"I can't explain someone else's actions, but if I had to hazard a guess, I would say he is doing it to put you on the back foot and make you question who you can trust. That gives him the opportunity to sweep in and take McPherson Financial Solutions business for himself while you flounder around wondering what happened," Max finally says.

I almost laugh. I don't know what I was expecting, but it as sure as hell wasn't that.

Chapter 34
Cullen

"Wow. You are brazen," I say. I don't laugh, but I do shake my head in wonder. "In a grudging way, I almost admire the sheer balls it takes to sit there and not only lie to my face, but to then have the sheer audacity to look angry at me."

"I still don't know what the hell you are getting at here Cullen so instead of sulking and making half accusations, can you please just tell me what the hell it is that you think I've done?" Max says, her snapping tone matching her angry expression.

Fuck it. I'll tell her exactly what she's done.

"Bill didn't lie about getting an email. He knew every detail of the proposal down to the price I was charging and why I was offering such a big discount. And he told me the email was sent from you," I tell her.

"And you just believed him?" Max says, doing a decent impression of a shocked expression.

"Of course not," I say.

I'm well aware that I don't need to explain myself to her

at this point, not after what she has done to me both person-ally and professionally, but I also want her to know that I didn't automatically think the worst of her, that I did at least consider the fact that Bill could be lying for some nefarious purpose, much like the excuse she gave me earlier where she said he might be doing it to get in my head and distract me from the end goal. Max raises an eyebrow like she doesn't believe I would question it, and although I again tell myself that I don't need to prove myself to her, I find myself explaining what happened just the same.

"I gave you the benefit of the doubt and told him to prove it. He forwarded the email to me and then I couldn't tell myself he was lying anymore after that. I don't get it Max. What did I ever do to you that made you want to destroy me like that? I gave you a job when no one else would, and you sell me out like that. What did he offer you? Extra money? A company car? Better annual leave? What? And you know what? I couldn't have forgiven you, but I could have shrugged it off as it being business and some people can't be trusted. But you would have gotten inside information like that about the company without you worming your way into my bed as well as my office," I say.

I didn't mean to let the hurt show, but I can't help it. At least I said bed and not heart. Max is looking at me like I'm crazy again and it makes it worse that even now with the evidence lined up against her and the damage done, she still wants to keep up her story.

"Are you fucking kidding me Cullen? It's bad enough that you think I would leak company information to anyone, but for you to actually think I would seduce you just to play with you. What sort of a person do you think I am?" Max demands.

For a moment, I pause, not wanting to go down this path, but no. I will have my say. After what she's done, she doesn't get to sit there now and take the moral fucking high ground.

"I don't know anymore. I thought I knew you, but obviously I didn't know you at all. You know, you shouldn't be wasting your time working for me or Bill Bryson. You should be an actress because by God you are good," I say.

"It's easy to act innocent when you are innocent," Max says.

I don't know why it keeps surprising me that she's still sticking to her story, but it does. I figured there would come a point where she would have to admit defeat and just admit what she had done, but it seems that nope, it's not going to come to that. I wonder if I had footage of her sending the email – which I obviously don't – that she would still try to say it wasn't her, that the cameras were somehow wrong. Probably if her insistence on her lie right now is anything to go by.

I have had enough of this dance now and I no longer need her to admit the truth to me. I have accepted that isn't going to happen, and I will learn to make my peace with it. I just need her out of my office and out of my life.

"You know what? I'm done. You're not going to have the balls to admit to my face what you've done, so whatever, go and slither off and find someone who employs snakes, because you've shot yourself in the foot at Cyber Safe, they don't work like that. And you've certainly shot yourself in the foot with me. You're fired Max. Get your stuff and leave immediately. And get your stuff out of my house before I finish here today because anything of yours left behind will be getting thrown into the trash," Cullen says.

I watch Max as the mask of anger slips off her face, and instead, she looks upset. Tears come to her eyes and start to roll down her face. At first, it sends a pang of pain through my heart to see her crying, and it takes everything I have not to go to her and hold her, but I stop myself. She is playing me still and I'm still falling for it. I roll my eyes like there was never any danger of it working on me.

"Save the water works for someone who hasn't seen through your bullshit," I snap.

I was probably harsher in my tone than I meant to be, but I'm fed up with her taking me for a fool and maybe it's about time she knows that her actions will have consequences, including me telling her it like it is.

My harsh tone seems to get the message through in a way my questions didn't penetrate, because Max stands up finally. I remain sitting and wait for her to leave. She has one more parting shot before she leaves and she bends down slightly and puts her palms on my desk and then she looks me in the eye as she speaks and her voice, although slightly tearful, is clear and strong, and for a moment, she almost has me fooled once again.

"One day you will find out the truth of what happened with this," she tells me. "And you will learn that I did nothing wrong. When that happens, and you see what you've thrown away, I hope it hurts you even half as much as it's hurt me."

She doesn't give me a chance to reply to that -what would I say even if she did? She just turns away from me and storms off across my office to the door. She doesn't look back – she just leaves my office, slamming the door behind her, leaving me alone with nothing but the echo of her leaving my life.

I'm horrified to find that I'm close to tears myself as I watch her leave me, but I'm not going to let her do that to me. She has done enough bloody damage, caused me enough pain. I get up and go to the window and look outside, trying to calm myself down. It doesn't work and I turn around and slam my fist into the wall. It hurts like a bastard and when I look down, I have broken the skin on my knuckles, but I feel better, calmer, and the urge to cry seems to have gone away so I reckon that it was worth losing a few bits of skin over.

I stalk back to my seat and force myself to concentrate on that damned invoice I'm meant to be approving. I manage to get it done and I go to lift the receiver of my desk phone to find out what appointments I have today, but I stop, my hand hovering above the phone. Of course, there's no one to answer my call or my question.

I look for myself at my calendar and there is nothing pressing enough that it can't be rearranged, and I send a message to the main reception desk asking one of the recep-tionists to clear my schedule for the day as I'm going to be out of the office. I almost add a note to say Max had to go home sick because I know they'll be wondering why I'm asking them to do her work for her and I'm not ready to tell anyone she's been sacked because then they'll ask why, and I don't have the heart to talk about that today. I decide against the note. Let them wonder. It's my company and I don't owe anyone an explanation.

Chapter 35
Cullen

After five minutes, I get a message back saying my schedule is cleared and of course there is no note asking why I needed the task done by them. God, losing Max has really shaken me up. I have never before considered that someone might question why I need something done at work by them instead of someone else. And I have certainly never thought about explaining to the receptionists where my secretary is if she's not at her desk. But then again nothing like this that has rocked my world completely has ever happened, so I guess that makes sense.

I know I'm not going to get any work done today and I also know if I stay in the office, I will keep trying to do something useful rather than just sitting here staring into space, and I'm likely to fuck something up and I can really do without having to come in early tomorrow to fix whatever crap I cause today. I shut down my computer, grab my jacket, and leave the office. It's the best decision for me both personally and professionally.

It's only when I get in my car and start the engine up

that I realize I can't go home. Not yet. I told Max to go and get her shit from my house and the last thing I want to do is run into her there. I don't feel like eating so that rules out sitting in a restaurant and it's far too early in the day for me to be drinking or sitting in a bar so, where can I go?

I could go and see my mom, but she would ask questions and it would all come out about Max and me and she would be so excited that me and her best friend's daughter were a thing, but then when I told her how it ended, it would only upset her, and I don't want to risk ruining her friendship with Max's mom. It's not her fault things went to shit with us. I could go and see Liam and just tell him that I don't want to talk about what's wrong, and I know he would accept that and leave me to stew in silence, but I really don't want to be around anyone right now.

Usually, if I want to go somewhere quiet and think, I go to the little sandy beach on the banks of the river not far from home, but I have taken Max there now and I think that place is now ruined for me unfortunately. It certainly wouldn't be the place for me to sit and try not to think about Max. I would feel like I could see her sitting there beside me, hear her laughter, taste her kiss. It would be the opposite of what I want.

I could go to the gym or for a walk or something physical. That always helps when my mind is running a mile a minute, but I can't exactly do either of those things in my suit and work shoes, and I can't go home to change, because if I could go home, then I wouldn't have this problem at all.

In the end, I drive out to the nearest mall and sit in the parking lot for an hour. I would have just stayed in the office parking lot but that would have looked really weird to staff members and clients coming and going.

Finally, I think the time I have been away should be enough for Max to have been in and out of my place and I start my car's engine and head over there. If I see her car in the vicinity, I will just keep driving down my street and go somewhere else for a bit longer.

I get to my street and the coast is clear. I let myself into my house, stopping to pick up a key from the floor. Max must have been for her stuff then and given it back in when she was done. I drop the key in my jacket pocket, and then, despite already knowing she has been and gone, I still go upstairs and check in the bathroom. All of Max's stuff is gone and while that should please me and let me relax knowing I'm not going to be ambushed by her unexpectedly, it just makes me sad. It's a visual reminder that she's gone from my life.

I go into the bedroom and lay down on the bed. I curl up on my side and get comfortable. I don't know what I'm going to do for the rest of the day, but I figure if I'm just going to mope around thinking of Max – and that is looking pretty likely, I'll be honest - then I might as well be comfortable while I'm doing it. I close my eyes, thinking I might be able to have a nap, but sleep eludes me and all I see when I close my eyes is Max. Her smile, her laugh, the face she pulls when she is about to climax, the way her hips seem to have been made for my hands to hold onto, her beautiful breasts and of course, her pussy. How can I not think of that. How can I not think of the way it felt wrapped around my cock, and how it tightened when I made her come. How can I not think of how I told her that if I fucked her one more time, she was mine and how she agreed to the terms, knowing that she wasn't ever going to be mine. Not really.

I don't know how to stop thinking about her, but I figure having my eyes closed is making it easier for me to picture her and so I open them and concentrate on the pattern on my feature wall instead. It doesn't work. Of course it doesn't work. It was never going to work. I'm going to torment myself whether I'm lying down, sitting up, have my eyes open or my eyes closed. It's just the way I am. I will torment myself, obsess over every little detail of a thing until finally, I have picked it apart enough that I can let it go. I know this is what I do and yet I still try to fight the process and save myself the heartache.

I still find it so hard to align the Max who I was falling in love with and who I'm sure felt the same way about me, and the Max who would backstab me like this. I can't fathom out why she waited until now. OK, so the McPherson deal was a big deal, and I can understand why she took that opportunity when it came along, but it's not like she knew it was coming, so why did she wait? Why didn't she sell me out when she openly hated me rather than making me like her first? There were plenty of other smaller, but still more than respectable, client accounts she could have leaked.

It's like trying to make two different people into one. Maybe she has an evil twin I think to myself, but I don't laugh. I can't laugh because as absurd as that is, I still want it to be true. How fucking pathetic is that?

I sigh and force myself to stop trying to make excuses for Max, for either of her personalities. The thought of making two different personas into one whole person makes me think of something else, something I feel is important, but the thread of the thought drifts away from me before I can grasp it. I don't suppose it was anything other than my mind finding another way to torture me anyway. I should probably be grateful to just let it float away like that. But I can't quite let it go. I don't know why but I keep musing on it for a moment, but nope. Whatever it was that piqued my interest has gone and doesn't seem to be in any rush to be coming back.

I push the idea away, not wanting to be stuck with some mental equivalent of an ear worm – would that be called a brain worm or something else? - all day. I feel bad enough without letting something like that get underneath my skin too. I close my eyes again, sick of staring at the wall now, and I force myself to picture anything but Max's face or body or voice or any part of her.

Her face is replaced by two colorful circles in my mind's eye. The circles float over each other and then fit together in perfect harmony, two parts of one whole. I still don't know what this is trying to tell me, but it's distracting me in a fairly harmless way seeing shapes floating around and slotting together and I stop thinking and just watch the shapes float. It's actually kind of soothing.

Or at least it is until it hits me moments later what this is all about. I was thinking about there being two sides to Max – the one that loved me and the one that betrayed me. But it's not like I didn't know in advance that she was two personas. She was Lucy in the office and Max out of it.

That was the thread that has been tickling at me, and that's what those shapes represented, two sides of the same coin that put together so easily although on the surface, they appear to be different. I get that, but why it is significant I don't know. Maybe my brain is just trying to be all clever and drawing the comparison between her being so two-faced and her actually having two different personas. Except that doesn't feel right. And it still doesn't feel right that Max betrayed me. Despite the evidence, it just doesn't feel like something she would do. Would it be something that Lucy would do?

Oh no. I am not going there. I am not going to start to think that Max has some sort of split personality disorder and the Max I love and the Lucy that betrayed me are two different people living inside of the same body.

My rambling thoughts still try to tell me that these two things are linked, the idea of the shapes slotting together and Max and Lucy slotting together, but I don't know how, and I don't care. I'm done thinking, done analyzing, done trying to keep that spark of hope alive. I roll onto my back and stare up at the ceiling and then I close my eyes again.

It seems that all I needed to do to find out why these random thoughts keep niggling at me is to let them go, because out of nowhere, the answer slams into me and I sit up abruptly. Two halves of the same person – Lucy at work, Max everywhere else. Not two different personalities, but two identities. Two identities that Max made damned sure to keep separate from each other, and the email that Bill had sent me. I was sure it was ... could it be ... was it signed off as Max, because if it was, that would mean Max hadn't actually sent that email?

No. I'm clutching at straws again, and I have to let this go. The email was obviously signed off by Lucy or I would have noticed at the time (but would I? And why would Bill tell me the email was from Max if it was signed by Lucy? It's not like he knows her and knows her nickname) and I'm just seeing it in my head now as Max because that's how I think of her both in and out of the office. And lets' face it, now I have come up with this theory, it's what I want to see, what I want to believe. I am sure there is some logical explanation for Bill using the name Max not Lucy. I mean right now, if my life depended on it, I couldn't think of one, but that doesn't mean there isn't one.

It doesn't matter one way or the other now anyway, because for better or for worse, I have found my spark of hope still burning somewhere and I intend to cling to it and protect it. I'm not willing to let it go out until I'm certain I'm wrong, and the more I think about it, the more I don't think I am wrong. I get up and leave my bedroom. By the time I start down the stairs, I'm more convinced than ever that I'm right about this, and I'm jogging. I tell myself I can't put too much faith into this because if I allow myself to believe it whole heartedly and then I'm wrong, it will break my heart all over again. But it's too late for that. Adrenaline is pumping through my body, and I am a man on a mission now.

Chapter 36
Cullen

I dash out of the house and run to my car. I jump in, start the engine up and head back towards the office. I almost expected my car not to start but it did. And surprisingly, the traffic isn't that thick either. Is the universe actually on my side for once?

Maybe not, because of course it's typical that the one day I didn't bother to bring my work laptop home with me from the office because I was determined that I wouldn't need it is the one time I actually do need it. I think the universe just likes to fuck with me. It gives and it takes away and it gives, and it takes away and the cycle just repeats itself. I'm going to stop that cycle though. If I'm right about this, then I won't let the universe take Max away from me again.

I'm pretty sure that I break every speed limit there is to get back to the office and I come pretty close to running a red light, but I make it back to the office in record timing and in one piece. The universe took away from me by leaving my laptop at the office, but then it gave back to me by letting me get it without getting a ticket or totalling my car.

I'm not much liking these hippy dippy thoughts I'm having, but I can't seem to stop them. I guess that's what I get for wanting to think about anything but Max. Wish granted, think about crazy stuff instead and start to think it makes sense.

I park my car and jog to the building and across the lobby. I wait impatiently for the elevator. It finally comes and I go up and make my way to my office. I greet a few people as I make my way down the hallways but luckily no one wants to stop me to ask me anything or for a chat. I get to my office and go in and close the door behind me.

I go to my desk and sit down and look at my computer monitor. Now that I'm here, I'm almost afraid to look, because I have found it; the one spark of hope. And if I'm wrong about this, then it will be extinguished for good. But I have to know. I have to.

I open my emails and find the incriminating one from Bill Bryson. I open it up and I click to open the attachment and there it is. My stomach whirls and my heart skips a beat. I was right and it's there in black and white. The email is signed off by Max.

Max is two different personas in one person. Lucy at work and Max outside of the office. This email is signed off as Max. It really fucking is. I'm not seeing things or just having a moment of wishful thinking. If Max had really sent that email, it would have been signed off as being from Lucy. She was telling me the truth the whole time. She isn't a great actress – she genuinely had no idea what I was talking about. I don't think she was right about Bill

Bryson making this up though. The figures are all too accurate, and he wouldn't know my secretary's name, let alone her nickname. This has to be from someone who knows Max by her nickname but either doesn't know it isn't her real name or doesn't know she doesn't use it at work.

I don't have time to mull over any of that stuff now. It doesn't seem important when compared with what else I have to do. I have to get to Max's place and tell her how sorry I am that I didn't believe her. I have to win her back. I will get down on my knees and beg her to forgive me if I need to. I will do whatever it takes, give her whatever she asks for. I can't believe I didn't take her word for it when she said it wasn't her. But surely if she looks at it from my point of view, she will see why I did what I did. God, I hope so.

I jump back up and retrace my steps back to my car. I switch the engine on and head towards Max's apartment building. I push it, but I stay within the speed limits, or at least almost within them this time. I park my car up in Max's parking lot and run around to the front of her building. I don't bother ringing her intercom, knowing the door will be open anyway. If I give her a chance to send me away without me getting inside, I think at the moment, she might take it, but I think if I can just see her face to face, I can make this right. God, I hope I can.

I take the stairs two at a time and hurry towards Max's apartment. I reach out to knock on the door when I realize it's not actually closed all of the way. This sends a spike of concern through me. I know it's probably nothing, just an oversight as she came inside, but it's not like her to be so careless when it comes to security. I suppose it could be my fault, that she was upset because of what I said and that made her careless.

I don't know whether to knock or whether to just push the door open and announce myself. I'm debating it when I hear a voice from inside of Max's apartment. A male voice.

"I'm done being nice now. I am going to kiss you. You will kiss me back and then you will tell me that you love me. Or I will make you," the voice says.

I blink in shock. What the hell. Surely, she hasn't replaced me already. No, of course not, I tell myself, relief flooding through me. It's the TV. It has to be. I almost laugh at my own paranoia, but then the voice comes again. It has fallen to a whisper, but I still hear the words.

"Say it Max," the voice says.

It definitely isn't the TV then, because whoever it is in there is using Max's name. I almost turn and walk away but there is something menacing about the voice and some of the words make it sound almost like whoever is talking is trying to force themselves on Max. I know it probably isn't that, but I can wait another moment or two just to be sure.

"I will never say those words to you, Ross." This time the voice that has spoken belongs to Max. Ross. Who is Ross? I think, judging by what he is saying, that he might be her abusive ex-boyfriend. But how would he have found her? I want to go in there and find out, but if I do that and it's not her ex-boyfriend, I will look ridiculous, so I wait and listen some more. Max is talking again.

"Not because it's too soon, or because I'm afraid that I will scare you away. I won't say those words to you because they are simply not true. I don't love you. I love Cullen," she says.

She loves me. After everything, she fucking loves me. I could happily do a little dance, but I remind myself that Max could be in danger, and I stay alert and wait for the other voice to respond.

"You had better keep that name out of your damned mouth girl because you and him are done. You are with me now and nothing and no one will keep us apart this time," the male voice says.

My hand is reaching for the door almost of its own accord. How dare he speak to my woman that way. I will fucking kill him.

"Don't fucking test me here Max," the voice says as the door to the apartment opens all of the way.

A flash of red anger clouds my vision at the sight that meets me as I step into the apartment. Max is pressed up against the wall, her wrists held over her head with some guy pinning them in place with one hand. He has his toes on top of hers, probably to stop her from kicking him. And he is holding her face roughly and moving in to kiss her. Her eyes are closed, and tears run down her face. She is trying to turn her head away from him to avoid being in the path of his kiss, but he is holding her face too tightly for her to move her head.

I don't hesitate. I cross the floor in four strides, grab the back of the man's shirt collar and drag him backwards away from Max.

"What the fuck?" he says as I drag him off Max,

Her eyes fly open as she is released from the man's grip, and they widen in shock when they see me. I spin the man around and smash my fist into his mouth and nose. Blood explodes from his nostrils and his lips, and his hands start to come up towards his face as he staggers backwards. I punch him again, before he can get his hands to his bleeding nose, and he goes down, unconscious. I half hope he's dead for what he has done to Max. I ignore his fallen body and turn to her.

"Are you ok?" I ask.

"I ... Yes. I am now," she says.

Chapter 37
Cullen

She looks a bit dazed but otherwise ok, and I take her hand in mine and lead her to the couch. I use my other hand to pull my cellphone out and I dial nine one one as I sit Max down.

"Nine one one, what's your emergency," the dispatcher says.

"Hi. I'm at one twenty-two Westcoat Avenue. There is an intruder. I have put him down and I will restrain him until the police arrive. Please hurry," I say.

I pull the cellphone away from my face even though I can hear the dispatcher talking.

"Sir? Sir?" she says, and I press the screen and end the call.

I glance over at the man. He's still out cold. I look back at Max. She is sitting on the couch where I led her towards, her hands clenched together in front of herself, her eyes staring into space and tears dripping off her chin. I go to her bedroom and grab a fleecy grey blanket. I come back and wrap it around her shoulders. She looks up at me briefly and smiles.

"How did you know he was here?" she says.

My cellphone is ringing, and the man is starting to stir.

"Later. I'll explain everything later," I say.

I go to the man and kneel down with one knee in the small of his back. I pull his arms behind his back and hold them in place with one hand. With the other, I check my cellphone. As I suspected it's the dispatcher calling me back. I ignore the call. I don't want to stay on the line until the cops arrive because I might get distracted from making sure this bastard doesn't get to go anywhere. Plus, I'm hopeful they will be a bit quicker if they don't know for sure that the situation is still under control.

The man squirms beneath me and I yank his arms up and he makes a pained sound and stops fighting against me. I stay tensed and ready for him to try something, but he doesn't bother trying again. Funny how guys like him can only fight against women. The police finally arrive about ten minutes later, two officers, a man, and a woman.

Max and I seem to notice them in the doorway at the same time.

"Come on in," Max says, standing up.

The officers come in and look around. The female office goes to Max and gently sits her back down, and the male officer comes over to me.

"I'll take it from here," he says.

I nod and get out of his way. He takes over my position, but he doesn't cuff the intruder yet. I go and sit beside Max on the couch.

"I'm Officer Reynolds and my partner is Officer

Norman," the woman officer says. "Can you tell me what happened here?"

Max explains how she heard a knock on her door and how she thought it was me, so she opened it, only to find Ross, her abusive ex-boyfriend standing there. So, I was right about it being him. I feel strangely guilty hearing how she opened the door because she thought it was me there, although it was hardly my fault.

She goes on to say that he said he wanted to talk to her and how scared she was, so she played along but he saw through it and how he slapped her face. He is lucky the police are here when she says this because if they weren't I would have killed the bastard with my bare hands for that. She carries on and says how he was trying to kiss her against her will when I came in and pulled him off her.

I tell my version of the story, how her apartment door was slightly ajar, and how I heard voices, and I realized that Max was in trouble, so I pulled her attacker off her and decapacitated him and called for help.

"What about the main door. Why is that left unlocked?" Officer Reynolds asks.

"Don't ask," Max says. "It's been reported plenty of times."

"And what about your apartment door. Doesn't that lock either?" she says.

"Yes," Max says. "I opened it for Ross thinking it was Cullen and when Ross came in, he didn't close it properly. I left it because I had a feeling that things would get out of hand and I thought with the door open, someone might hear something if it went really too far and call the police."

Her voice sounds a bit shaky, and Officer Reynolds seems to notice it too because she looks at Max in concern.

"Do you need an ambulance ma'am; get you checked over?" Officer Reynolds says to Max. She shakes her head. "Are you sure? You could be in shock."

"Honestly, I'm ok," Max says. "I just want to curl up here and forget this ever happened."

Officer Reynolds looks unsure and while I would rather Max go and get checked over, it's obvious she doesn't want to go to the hospital, so I step in.

"I'll stay with her Officer. If she shows any symptoms of shock, I will take her to the emergency room myself," I say.

"Ok," Officer Reynolds says, perhaps realizing this is the best that she's going to get right now. "We'll arrest him and charge him. I'll need both of you to come to the station in the morning and give official statements."

"No problem," I say.

Max nods her agreement.

"Bring me your landlord's details and I'll see if I can't scare him into fixing that lock as well," Officer Reynolds says.

"I will, thank you," Max says.

At Officer Reynolds' nod, Officer Norman pulls out a pair of handcuffs which he expertly puts on Ross and then he gets up and drags Ross to his feet.

"I am arresting you on the suspicion of assault and attempted sexual assault. You have the right to remain silent; anything you say can and will be used against you in a court of law. You have the right to an attorney and if you can't afford one, one will be provided for you. Do you understand?"; Officer Norman says.

Ross nods miserably.

"Yes," he croaks out.

Officer Norman marches him towards the door.

"This isn't over Max," Ross says.

"Oh, I think you will very much find that it is," I say.

He ignores me, looking at Max who won't meet his eye.

"I'll come back for you," he says.

"Like hell you will," I snap.

I start to stand up, but Officer Reynolds shakes her head.

"Please don't make me arrest you. This one needs you right now," she says, nodding at Max.

She's right and being there for Max is more important to me than being some sort of macho thug. Ross won't be bothering Max for a while at least now.

I nod my head and sit back down, and Max and I watch in silence as Officer Norman pulls Ross out of the apartment and out of sight.

"See you both tomorrow," Officer Reynolds says, heading for the door.

"Yes. Thank you, Officer," I say.

"Thank you," Max echoes me.

Officer Reynolds leaves the apartment, and she takes special care to make sure the door lock catches, even shaking the door slightly to be sure it's shut properly. The door stops rattling and the apartment goes quiet and there is just me and Max and the huge fuck up I threw between us.

"How did you know he was here?" Max says again, breaking the silence.

"I didn't. I came to apologize to you," I say. I shuffle closer to her and pick up her hand and hold it between both of mine. The fact she doesn't pull her hand away from me gives me hope and I hurry to try and explain things to her and make it right. "I heard what you said to Ross. That you don't love him you love me. I want you to know that I love you too Max. So much. And I am so, so sorry that I doubted you."

Chapter 38
Cullen

She looks at me with a pained expression on her face.

"You didn't just doubt me. You outright accused me of sabotaging you and then lying to your face about it. Oh, and I'm pretty sure somewhere along the way you accused me of seducing you to further my plan to stab you in the back," she says.

"I know. I don't know what else to say except I am so sorry, and I will spend every day of the rest of my life making it up to you if you will let me," I say.

"You promised you would never hurt me, and you hurt me so bad," Max says.

"I know, but I don't know what else to say except to tell you how sorry I am," I say.

"I wasn't finished," Max says with a small smile. "You fucked up Cullen. Big time. But I think everyone deserves a second chance. But I want your word right now that you will never doubt me again. If I tell you something, you believe me, even if it sounds unlikely. And don't ever accuse me of trying to sabotage you again."

"You have my word," I say. "I promise."

"Then I guess you're forgiven," Max says. "Oh, on one condition. I want my job back."

"Done," I say laughing with the pure joy of knowing this amazing woman has found it in her heart to give me another chance.

"When I thought it was you at the door come to apologize, I already knew I would end up forgiving you, but I planned on making it a lot harder than this," Max says with a soft laugh. "And then Ross did what he did, and I don't know. That drama back at the office just seemed less important somehow, and us being together seemed bigger than some argument. I'm curious though. How did you finally work out I was telling the truth?"

"Part of me knew it all along," I say. "But I convinced myself that was just wishful thinking because I didn't want it to be true, so I ignored that voice."

"I get that," Max admits. "And to be honest, I can see why you believed it was me because even knowing it wasn't me, I couldn't think of a better explanation."

"After I sent you home, I couldn't focus and so I went home myself and I was thinking and it occurred to me that it was strange that at first when you started working here, we didn't exactly like each other and yet you didn't do anything to stab me in the back then. I asked myself why you would wait until we were together to do it and I kept coming up blank. Anyway, it finally hit me that the email Bill forwarded to me was signed off as Max and that you use Lucy on all of your work correspondence," I say.

After I tell her this, I wonder if I should have lied and told her I just knew it in my heart, but I don't want to lie to her, even if the truth gets me in more trouble.

Max slaps herself in the forehead.

"Oh my God of course. I didn't even think of that myself," she says.

"We make a right pair, don't we?" I say.

I'm laughing but when Max looks at me and says yes, she is deadly serious and instantly I feel the mood of the room change and I feel my cock waking up. I want so badly to kiss her, but I don't know if she's ready for that after what happened with Ross.

"What's wrong?" Max asks when it becomes clear to her that I'm not about to make a move on her.

"Nothing," I say. "I just didn't know if it was too soon after him putting his hands on you. I don't want to like traumatize you or something."

"You got here just in time," Max says. "The most he managed to do was kiss my cheek where I turned my head away. I do feel kind of dirty just from being around him though. I need to shower before we do anything. Wait here?"

I nod my head and Max gets up. She heads to the door that leads to the small hallway that her bedroom and bathroom open off of and when she reaches it, she grins at me over her shoulder.

"Or don't," she says and winks at me and I know an invitation when I hear one.

I get up and follow her and by the time we get into the bathroom, we are both naked, a trail of our clothes leading to the shower stall. We step into it and Max turns the water on and adjusts the temperature. She stands under the flow of the water and turns her face up to the spray. I watch the water hit her skin and beads of it run down her back, over her ass cheeks and down her legs. She grabs her shower gel and soaps her skin and I watch her, my cock hard at the sight of her hands rubbing over her body. When I can't take the sight anymore, I move closer and begin to rinse her down with my hands. She moans as I pay particular attention to her breasts and nipples, and she leans back against me as my hands work their way down her belly and then one goes between her legs.

"It's very important this part is rinsed super thoroughly," I say.

"Oh, I agree," Max says as I rub my finger back and forth across her clit.

I work her and she moans and squirms against me. When she comes, she cries out and presses her ass against my hard cock, teasing me. I rub her inner thighs as she comes and when her orgasm fades away, she looks over her shoulder and grins at me.

"I think my clit is rinsed clean now, but I'm not sure about my pussy. I think you need to rinse it out with your ... ahem ... hose," she says, and she grabs my cock and gives it a squeeze making it very clear what she means by my hose.

Not one to disappoint, I push her forwards, bending her over. She braces herself against the shower wall and spreads her legs. Her pussy is dripping, a mixture of the shower water and her juices, and her mound is spread open, showing the pink swollen flesh of her lips. She looks amazing and she is all mine.

I take my cock in my hand and place it against her

pussy, and then I push myself inside of her. I thrust into her in hard, fast strokes that she matches, pushing herself back onto me, making each stroke seem deeper and deeper. When I'm on the verge of coming, I pull out of Max and spin her around. I grab her ass and lift her up and she wraps her legs around my waist and her arms around my shoulders and I slip back inside of her. She leans down and kisses me deeply as I begin to move inside of her again. After a moment, she pulls her mouth from mine and gasps as we hit our stride and within seconds, we are both hitting our climax. I bury my face in between Max's breasts as I come hard and she clings to me, her fingers digging into the backs of my shoulders as she whimpers my name.

Pleasure fills me and, in that moment, I know I have everything I have ever wanted. I hold Max a little bit tighter as my cock slips out of her and I set her back down on her feet, but I keep my arms around her, and she keeps hers around me.

"I love you Max," I say.

"I love you too," she says.

She leans her head back and I move my face down to hers and I kiss her, a kiss full of love and passion and a promise for the future. She kisses me back, her kiss as enthusiastic as mine and then we break apart. We get a final rinse down and then Max turns the water off and we get out of the shower, each of us wrapping ourselves in a towel. Max leads me to the bedroom and finds herself a pair of pajamas made up of a pair of shorts and a vest top in a lilac color. She holds out a pink robe to me.

"I'm sorry. It's the best I can do," she says.

"I'm comfortable enough with my masculinity to wear a

pink robe," I say with a laugh.

I put it on and then sit on the bed while Max puts her pajamas on and brushes her hair. We go back out into the living room.

"I'm starving," Max says. "Do you fancy some dinner? I'll see what I have in the frig."

"I'll order pizza," I say.

"Ok," Max agrees. "Pepperoni and mushroom?"

I nod my agreement and get my cellphone and open my food delivery app. I order the pizza and tell Max it's done.

"I was just thinking. It reminded me with us getting food delivered. Maybe one good thing will come out of the Ross thing. I think if Officer Reynolds calls my landlord, it might just scare him into fixing the door lock when he hears what happened," she says.

"I hope so because I hope the next tenant feels safe," I say. "But you're not staying here Max."

"Let's see what happens first. Maybe Ross will go to prison, and I won't need to move straight away," she says.

"No Max, you don't understand," I say. "For the past few weeks, I've been trying to find the right time to ask you to move in with me, and I haven't found it. But after everything that has happened, I'm done waiting. You're moving in with me."

"So, you decided instead of asking me, you would just demand it of me," she says, but there's a sparkle in her eye and I know she's joking so I nod my head.

"Yup. It's a done deal," I say.

"Yeah, I'd say you were right there," she says.

"Is that a yes then?" I press her.

"Even though you technically didn't ask, yes it's a yes,"

she says, and I grin and pull her to me and kiss her again.

"You make me happier than I ever thought I could be," I say.

She snuggles against me.

"I don't want to ruin the mood, but I keep thinking of that email. Who would want to split us up?" she says.

"You think that's what it was? An attempt to split us up rather than an attempt to sabotage the deal with Mr McPherson?" I say.

"I don't know for sure, but it seems that way. If someone else got access to the proposal and wanted to use it for personal gain, they would have had to put their name to it. If they just wanted to sabotage the deal, they could have sent it anonymously. Putting my name on it feels personal," Max says.

I think for a moment and nod my agreement. Now that she's mentioned it, I think she's right. But I have no idea who it could be.

"As far as I know, no one at work even knows I go by Max," Max says. "Except you obviously."

"And I am always careful not to call you Max around clients or other staff members," I say. "So, by that logic, it has to be someone from outside of work who doesn't know that you go by your real name in the office."

"But how would anyone from outside of work know about the proposal and who to send it to, let alone be able to actually get their hands on a copy," Max says. "Wait. Could it be a leak from McPherson's themselves? Maybe it's a way to get a better deal for them. And the person who sent it just so happens to be called Max. I know it's a long shot, but it's possible right?"

"I find it unlikely to be honest," I say. "It wasn't the neat copy we sent the client. It was a rough version, like the one where you transcribed the recording but hadn't finalized it."

"That makes no sense," Max says. "No one had access to the first draft of that except for me."

"Unless it is someone who works for the company and some how they've found out you go by Max and fucked up and signed the email that way, because someone at work could potentially have gotten onto your computer," I say.

"Can I see it?" Max says. "The email from Bill. Well, more the attachment."

"Of course," I say. "I don't have my works laptop with me though. You can see it tomorrow at the office after we give our statements to the police."

"Ok. Are you worried about giving a statement? In case you get charged with punching Ross?" Max says.

"The only thing I'm worried about in regard to that creep is that I didn't hit the fucker harder," I say.

Max picks my hand up and gently runs her finger over my grazed knuckles.

"I don't know. Your knuckles suggest you got a decent punch in," she says.

I laugh.

"What?" Max says,

"As much as I'm happy for you to think I'm some sort of macho guy that punched your ex hard enough to split my knuckles open, in the interest of total honesty, I must confess that I punched the wall at the office after our talk this morning," I say.

"Not your brightest move," Max says, and we both laugh.

A knock sounds on the door.

"That'll be the pizza," I say.

I get up and go and open the door, but it's not the pizza delivery guy. It's Harriet. She looks shocked to see me.

"What the fuck are you doing here?" she says. Before I can answer, she smirks. "Nice robe."

Fuck. I forgot about the robe. Oh well. She goes and sits down on the arm chair at the end of the couch.

"Max? Are you ok?" she asks. "I got your text after I finished work and came straight over. Looks like I was a bit late to the party though."

"I'm sorry," Max says as I retake my seat on the couch. "It was all a misunderstanding and everything is fine. I forgot I texted you or I would have let you know."

"Too busy kissing and making up?" Harriet says with a grin, and I realize then two things. One, why she's here and two, why she was so shocked to see me here. Max obviously texted her earlier and told her that we broke up.

"Partly," Max grins and then she turns serious. "But also, Ross turned up here."

"Oh fuck. What happened? How did he find you? Are you alright?" Harriet says.

I can't keep up with her questions, but Max seems to be able to do so without any problems.

"He followed you until one day you came here," she says. Harriet looks horrified and opens her mouth to speak, but Max waves her words away. "It's not your fault before you say anything. He barged in and honestly, I think he's lost his grip on reality a bit. He kept saying things like he would forgive me for seeing Cullen behind his back and he wouldn't accept we weren't together anymore. He started getting a bit handsy but then Cullen arrived and dealt with him. He punched him and knocked him unconscious. And yes, I'm fine."

Harriet looks at me.

"I was pissed you'd hurt my best friend, but she seems to have forgiven you so whatever. You get a pass for punching Ross. But I am gutted I wasn't here to see it," she says.

"It was brilliant," Max says. "His nose bled and then he went down like a sack of potatoes."

I love that Max loves how I punched Ross out and hearing her tell the story to her friend makes me feel kind of good. I'm not someone who goes around fighting, but if anyone lays a finger on my lady, they are going to know about it.

Another knock sounds on the door.

"This has to be the pizza this time," Max says.

I get up and go to the door again. This time, it is the pizza guy. He hands me the pizza and a bag with fries and another with a bottle of soda. I thank him and take the food and close the door.

"I should go, let you two have dinner in peace," Harriet says.

"Don't be silly, stay and eat with us," I say.

"Yeah stay," Max says. "Look at all of that. There's far too much for just the two of us."

"Well, if you're sure," Harriet says and we both nod.

"It'll be nice to get to know you better Harriet," I say.

"Yeah, especially now that we're going to be living together," Max adds.

"Oh wow, congratulations both of you," Harriet says.

She pulls Max into a hug over the chair arm. "I'm so happy and pleased for you."

I leave them to chat while I go to the kitchen area and grab three glasses for the soda and a handful of napkins. I come back to the coffee table and pour sodas for the three of us and we dig in. It's nice getting to know Harriet. She's funny and I can see why my brother was so taken with her that night we ran into Max and her friends in the club.

After we have eaten, Harriet takes her leave and Max and I snuggle up together again.

"You do realize you opened the door to the pizza delivery guy and Harriet in my pink robe, don't you?" Max says.

"Yeah," I say with a grin. "It was either that or be naked. Harriet might not have minded, but I think the pizza guy would have."

Max giggles and shakes her head.

"You're terrible," she says.

"Well, it won't be a problem after today," I say. "Because after work tomorrow, we are coming here and packing your stuff up and moving you into my place where I will always have a suitably masculine robe to put on."

Max stands up and holds her hand out to me. I take it and she pulls me to my feet.

"If this is going to be my last night in this bed, I think we should at least make the most of it, don't you," she says.

"Oh, most definitely," I agree.

I reach out and pinch her ass cheek and she lets out a squeal and runs. I chase her into the bedroom, and we fall onto the bed laughing and kissing.

Chapter 39

Max

I sit in Cullen's chair at his computer. He stands behind me, one hand on the back of the chair and the other one moving the mouse. He clicks around and opens the email from Bill Bryson.

"Do you want to read it?" he asks.

I shake my head. I want to see the attachment. If there is going to be any clues about who wanted to split me and Cullen up and also potentially cost him a client, they will be in the email I supposedly sent.

Cullen clicks the attachment and confirms he wants to open it. The attachment opens and fills the screen.

"Wrong one," Cullen says, moving the mouse towards the red x.

"Wait," I say. He stops moving the mouse. "Cullen, what's this?"

"I opened the wrong attachment," he says. "Instead of the copy of the email you wanted to see, this is a copy of the attachment sent with the original email."

I don't reply as I stare at the document in front of me.

"But ..." I start and then stop again.

Cullen laughs and I feel his breath on my ear as he moves in and quickly pecks my cheek.

"You've only been gone a day Max. Surely you recognize your own notes," he says.

"That's just it though," I reply. "Cullen these aren't my notes."

"Are you sure? Because everything on that document checks out in terms of the figures and the recommendations I made," Cullen says.

"I'm sure," I say.

"I'm not doubting you Max, but how can you be so sure? You haven't had time to read more than a line or two," Cullen says.

Even as he says it, I'm scanning the document, reading more of it, but that's only to satisfy my own curiosity about whether or not Cullen is right that the document is factually correct. I already know for certain that it isn't a copy of my notes.

"My notes were hand-written," I say, still reading.

"What?" Cullen says.

I stop reading. I've seen enough to know what I think has happened here. I spin the chair slightly so that I'm facing Cullen.

"When I was transcribing the audio file from the meeting with Mr McPherson, my computer was taking forever to switch between the file and the Word document I was using to take notes on. In the end, I decided it would be easier to make hand-written notes and type those up instead of keeping having to stop and start the playback of the file,"

I say. "These facts and figures are accurate, but they aren't mine."

"Why didn't you say this yesterday?" Cullen says. "It would have proved your innocence."

"Because I didn't realize the attachment you had been sent was typed up. When I finished making my notes, I scanned the sheets of paper I used onto my computer. I assumed that you had been sent a copy of that," I tell him.

"I see," he says and then he goes quiet for a moment. "This narrows down our suspects somewhat. It has to be someone from here who was able to get into your computer to get the audio file to work from."

"Or anyone who potentially had access to my cell-phone," I point out.

"It would have had to have been between the meeting with Mr McPherson ending at ..." Cullen says. "Can you open the calendar and work it out?"

"Sure," I say.

I do as he asks.

"Eleven twenty seven Tuesday morning," I say.

"Right. And I received the email from Bill at ..." Cullen is back to moving the mouse and looking over my shoulder at the computer monitor. "Nine fourteen Wednesday morning. And that was about ten minutes after he called me, so let's say nine o'clock Wednesday morning. Obviously, the person would have needed time to do the notes from the audio file, but let's just disregard that for now because we don't know their skill level to know how fast or slow that was. So, I will look at the sign in records and make a list of everyone who had access to your computer between the hours of eleven twenty seven on Tuesday morning and nine fourteen Wednesday morning. Can you do the same but for who might have had access to your cellphone, but obviously don't include anyone who works here because I'll have them on my list, unless of course it was a social visit, and they weren't at work that day."

I give Cullen his chair back and go around to the other side of the desk. I pick up the note pad and pen off the desk and sit thinking about where I had been between those hours. Cullen was clicking around on his computer as I pondered it.

We had come straight back here after the meeting and my lunch break had been spent in the staff breakroom with Cullen. After work, I left with him and went straight back to his place and I didn't see anyone else until I came back to work the next morning, which was the day I took a half-day meaning the email had been sent before I even left Cullen's house.

I jump a bit when the printer whirs into life in the corner of Cullen's office. He gets up and goes to it and comes back with two sheets of paper, each covered with a list of names.

"Where's your list?" he says.

"Outside of the office, I was only with you," I say. "I think we can rule you out, but for argument's sake, you're on that list anyway."

"So somewhere on this list is our culprit," Cullen says and then he grins. "God listen to me saying words like culprit."

"I think visiting the police station this morning has gone to your head, and turned you into a bit of a detective," I say with a giggle.

We had been to the police station first thing to give our statements about yesterday with Ross. God I can't believe that was only yesterday. It already feels like a lifetime ago. Officer Reynolds had taken my statement and Officer Norman had taken Cullen's, and afterwards, Officer Reynolds confirmed that no charges would be pressed against Cullen because they deemed that he had used reasonable force to detain the man. I was glad that part was over, but Officer Reynolds had warned that if Ross pleaded not guilty and the whole thing had to go to trial both Cullen and I would be called on to testify against him.

"Let's play cop then and go through this list," Cullen says pulling me back out of my thoughts and back into the moment. I nod my head in agreement and Cullen gets his chair and wheels it around to my side of the desk. He spreads page one of the list of names down in the middle of us. "Let me know if anyone in particular jumps out at you."

I read down the first page and shake my head. I recognize most of the names as people who work here, and there are a few names I don't recognize who I figure work in a department I have never really had any interaction with. Cullen switches the page for page two. I scan through the list and point to one of the names there: Kimberly Trent.

"Her?" Cullen asks and I shake my head quickly.

"No. I mean we can rule her out," I say.

"Are you sure?" Cullen asks.

I nod my head.

"Yes," I say. "Other than my lunch break, which I spent with you, I went to the bathroom twice and had a five minute coffee break. On each occasion, she was there when I was, and we were laughing about who was stalking who."

"Ok," Cullen says. "Fifty-nine names and we have managed to eliminate one. And no one jumps out at you as suspicious or someone who you don't get along with?"

I shake my head.

"No, sorry," I reply. "Hey, you don't have a secret house-keeper who is madly in love with you and makes trouble for all of your girlfriends do you?"

"I'm afraid not," Cullen laughs. "That would have made everything so much easier, wouldn't it?"

"It sure would," I agree. Then something comes to me. "Oh wait. I think we can eliminate Sandra from reception too. She came to see me about something, and I had head-phones on, and she asked what I was listening to, and I told her what I was doing. and she could see me using a pen and paper at the time. So, if it was her, she wouldn't have made a typed version of the notes."

"Two down, fifty-seven to go," Cullen says.

"Maybe the IT department can help," I say. "If Bill Bryson is willing to let one of your guys look at the email on his computer, they might be able to work out where it was sent from. Like as in which computer if it's one in the office."

"It could work. Let me get onto IT and ask them if that's possible and if so, I'll give Bill a call and see if he's willing to work with us," Cullen says.

"Sounds good," I say and then I get up. "I really must go back to work. I've already had a late start today."

Cullen nods and I go out of his office and to my desk and start on my work. Most of my stuff is back in place and the space feels like mine again. I settle down and get engrossed in my work. After I have been working for almost an hour, my cellphone rings. I glance at the screen and see a local number I don't recognize. I almost ignore the call as I generally do with numbers I don't recognize, but with it being a local number, I decide to see who it is. I pick it up and poke at the answer option on the screen.

Chapter 40
Max

"Hello," I say bringing the cellphone up to my ear.

"Am I speaking to Lucy Granger?" a female voice asks.

I feel like I vaguely recognize the voice, but I can't place it. I wonder if it's my doctor's office or dentist or something with them using my formal name.

"Yes," I say.

"How are you, Lucy? This is Officer Reynolds," the voice says.

"Oh. hi Officer," I say. "Is everything ok?"

"Yes, nothing to worry about," Officer Reynolds says. "I was wondering if it would be ok if I stopped by for a quick chat?"

"Yes, of course," I say. "I'm at work but it's fine to stop by here." I give her the address. "I'll let reception know I'm expecting you."

"Ok, see you soon," Officer Reynolds replies and ends the call.

I make a quick call down to reception as promised and of course I get asked what I've done to warrant a visit from the police. I don't really want everyone here knowing my business, but I don't want to seem like I don't want to be friendly with people either, so I respond by laughing and saying, "wouldn't you like to know?".

Despite Officer Reynolds assuring me the visit is nothing to worry about, I can't help but keep thinking about it. What could she possibly want since this morning? I didn't know but I figured if either Cullen or I were in trouble, she probably wouldn't warn us she was coming. I had probably missed a signature on my statement or something and she was stopping by because it would get done quicker that way than waiting for me to go back down to the station. Yeah, that's probably it, I tell myself, but I still find it difficult to concentrate on my tasks because I keep thinking about other possibilities, none of them nice ones.

Luckily, I don't have too long to wait before I look up and see Officer Reynolds and Officer Norman heading along the hallway towards me. They reach my desk, and we make the appropriate greetings.

"Is there somewhere private we can talk?" Officer Reynolds asks.

I think for a moment and then I stand up.

"I'll ask Cullen if we can use his office," I say.

Officer Reynolds nods her head and I go and knock on Cullen's office door.

"Come in," he calls.

I go in.

"Officer Reynolds and Officer Norman are here to talk

to me about something," I say. "Can we use your office please?"

"Of course," Cullen says.

"Thanks," I say.

I open the door and let the officers know we can use the room. They come in and greet Cullen who shakes both of their hands and grabs his cellphone.

"I'll get out of your way," he says. "I'll be in conference room C if you can let me know when you're done."

"No, you don't have to go," I say. I look at Officer Reynolds. "Right?"

"He can stay if you want him to," she confirms.

I nod my head at Cullen. I do want him to stay.

"Ok, I'll stay," he says. He nods towards the table with six chairs around it at one end of his office. "Why don't we take a seat at the table? Can I offer either of you any refreshments?"

Both of the officers decline a drink, and we all go and sit down at the table. Cullen puts his hand on my knee beneath it and gives it a reassuring squeeze.

"We wanted to let you know personally that Ross Baker has taken a plea agreement," Officer Reynolds says,

"You mean he admitted hitting me?" I say.

"Yes, and not just that either," Officer Reynolds says. "As you know from when we arrested Mr Baker, we planned on charging him with assault and attempted sexual assault. His lawyer took a plea offer to the DA's office where Mr Baker pleaded guilty to the assault and one count of hacking ..."

"Hacking?" I say interrupting without thinking.

"Yes. Mr Baker admitted to hacking your cellphone,"

Officer Reynolds says. "He was able to access any text messages, direct messages sent through any social media network, emails, and voice mails. Pretty much the only things he couldn't listen in to were your phone calls and video calls."

I glance at Cullen and it's clear from his expression that he has understood the same thing as I have. It was Ross who took the notes from the audio file and sent them to Bill Bryson. Ross who we now know had access to the file and who most definitely wanted Cullen and me to break up. It also explains something else for me – how he knew so quickly that Cullen and I had split up and that I had been fired. Maybe if I had thought more on that we would have worked out it was Ross sooner, but it wouldn't have been much sooner so as it stands; it really wouldn't have made any difference.

"The maximum custodial sentence for hacking is two years and with the assault, we might have gotten two and a half," she says. "The attempted sexual assault was going to be the hardest bit to prove, but also the most damaging for Mr Baker going forward. So, his plea bargain basically said he would do two years in prison and in exchange, we drop the attempted sexual assault charges. He will still be listed as someone who has been violent to women, but he won't go on the sex offenders register."

I take a moment to process everything Officer Reynolds has told me. I'm more than happy with the outcome. If it had gone to court, it would have dragged on and on and I would have had to testify which I was dreading. And he likely would have gotten a similar sentence anyway, because there was always going to be reasonable doubt about the attempted sexual assault because with no witnesses, it was just a case of he said she said. And when I thought about it, Ross had been violent to me and abusive yes, but he had never done anything sexually and I don't think for a second that he was getting off on hitting me.

While I didn't like him trying to kiss me against my will and I do class it as sexual assault of a kind, I don't think Ross is likely to be a danger to women in the sense of him being a sexual predator, so if justice being done means he isn't going to be put on the sex offenders register, but will be officially someone who has been found guilty of domestic violence, then I can live with that.

"So, it's over?" I say after a few minutes.

"For you, yes," Officer Reynolds says.

"But for that bastard, it's only just beginning," adds Officer Norman with a smile.

"Thank you," I say. "Both of you. For dealing with this so quickly and keeping Ross off the streets, and also for letting me know straight away. It's certainly a weight lifted off my mind."

We all say our goodbyes and shake hands and then the two officers leave, and Cullen and I are alone together.

"Are you ok?" Cullen says. "I know that was good news, but it's still a lot to take in."

"Yes, I'm ok. Just processing it all, I guess. I can't believe I have two years where I don't have to worry about Ross finding me," I say.

Cullen comes over to me and wraps his arms around me and kisses the top of my head.

"You never have to worry about Ross finding you again,

because if he comes within ten feet of you, I will end him," he says.

I squeeze Cullen tightly. I know he means what he says and that he won't let Ross hurt me again and for the first time in a long time, standing there in the arms of the man I love, I feel safe.

* * *

The work day has pretty much ended, and I go to Cullen's office. I tap on his door and he calls out for me to come in.

"I won't be a minute," he says. "I'm almost done."

I sit down to wait for him, and he really is only a few seconds before he closes his laptop with a flourish.

"Done," he says. "Let's go."

"Actually, there's something I wanted to talk to you about first," I say.

"Oh, that sounds ominous," Cullen says with a laugh. When I don't laugh too, he frowns at me. "Are you ok?"

"Yes," I say. "I just ... I know you only said I should move in with you today because you were scared that I was in danger from Ross. Well now I'm not, so I just wanted you to know that if you want to change your mind, I get it."

"Do you not want to move in with me Max?" Cullen says.

"Yes, I do," I say. "But I get it if it's too soon for you. That's all I'm saying. I don't want you to feel like you have to do something when the circumstances that brought that something about have changed."

"I want to live with you Max. When I said I have wanted to live with you for a while and I was trying to find the perfect time to ask you to move in with me, I wasn't just saying that because of the situation," Cullen says. "Granted if Ross hadn't been a danger to you, I probably wouldn't have booked a moving company for this evening. I likely would have waited until the weekend when we had a bit more time, but that's the only thing I would have changed."

I feel relief flood me. It only occurred to me a couple of hours ago that Ross being behind bars where he belongs might change things for Cullen and me and I have been worrying about it ever since, but I knew I had to give him the chance to get out of this, and now I'm really glad I did, because I know now that Cullen hasn't just gone through with this out of a sense of obligation to me. He really does want to live with me.

I smile at Cullen, and he smiles back and comes around the desk to me and pulls me to my feet. He kisses me and then he grins at me.

"Come on, let's go home. Together. To our home," he says, and he takes my hand, and we walk out of the office together and into our shared future.

Epilogue

M^{ax}

Christmas Eve, Six Months After Max Moved in with Cullen.

"Are we mad?" I say and not for the first time as I look at the pile of wrapped presents beneath our giant green Christmas tree and think of the hours of prep we have done for Christmas dinner tomorrow.

"I think we might be," Cullen says with a laugh.

It's our first Christmas together and instead of spending it just the two of us as we first discussed, our plans changed mid-December when both of us told our moms we wouldn't be home for Christmas and both of them were upset about it. We talked about it, and we decided that we would host Christmas for both of our families so that we could be together on the day and no one else missed out on our company.

It started off just my mom, Cullen's mom, and Liam. Now Harriet and Sam and her husband are joining us too.

"I guess that's what Christmas is all about though," I say.

"What? Going mad?" Cullen says.

"No," I say laughing. "Family and friends coming together to celebrate."

"That's not what you said when you forced me to buy the matching pajamas," Cullen says. "You said then it was all about getting into the Christmas spirit and having fun."

"Well, that's almost the same thing isn't it," I say. I look at him in his elf pajamas and smile. "And you can't say you don't look adorable in them."

"Oh, trust me, I can," Cullen laughs. "Now let's enjoy the calm before the storm tomorrow is going to bring."

He lifts his arm up and I move along the couch until I'm tucked snugly underneath it, and we snuggle in. Cullen hits play on the remote and I smile as Home Alone, my favorite Christmas movie of all time, starts to play.

This really is perfect I think to myself. The decorations are up, the tree lights are twinkling, I have a nice glass of wine and my favorite Christmas movie on, and I'm getting to share it all with the love of my life. It's not everyone who has so much to be happy about and I'm so grateful for everything this year has brought me, even if it was a slightly bumpy road to get here.

"Right. Out with it. What's going on? Why are you so

nervous?" I say when Cullen excuses himself to go to the bathroom for the third time in the first hour of the movie.

"Who said I'm nervous?" Cullen says as he heads for the stairs.

"Umm, your bladder," I say, and he laughs.

I pause the movie and wait for him to come back down the stairs. He does and he looks even more on edge than ever. He sits down and then he gets up and fills both of our wine glasses and then he sits down again.

"Ok, you're fidgeting now. There's definitely something going on. Look if you've planned some sort of surprise party or something, please tell me so that I can go and get changed," I say.

"You honestly think I would be wearing these if I thought people were coming over," Cullen laughs.

"Ok, fair point," I say. "But seriously, what's wrong?"

I have never seen Cullen so on edge before and his nerves are starting to make me feel nervous too.

"I have a present for you, one that I want to give you early, but I'm afraid that you won't like it," he says.

"I'm sure I will like it," I say.

"Ok. Well here goes," he says.

He puts his hand into his pajama pants pocket and pulls out a small red package covered in sticky tape.

"The lady in the shop offered to gift wrap it for me, and like a fool I said no. I thought wrapping it myself would somehow make it more special. I see now that I made a really bad choice there," he says, and we both laugh.

"Don't worry," I say. "The wrapping paper is only going to get torn off and thrown away anyway."

He gives me the little present and I get stuck trying to

tear the paper and tape off. I get it open and it's a little blue velvet gift box. I go to open the box, but Cullen puts his hand over mine and stops me. I look at him questioningly and he smiles nervously and then he stands up and drops to one knee before me, and suddenly I know what is in the little blue box.

Cullen gently takes the box from me and then he looks up at me and smiles and it seems like all his nerves have just dropped away.

"Max, I love you and I will love you forever. Having you in my life filled a hole I didn't even know I had, both in my life and in my heart. I want to spend forever trying to make you as happy as you make me every day of my life. What I'm trying to say is Max Granger, will you marry me?" Cullen says.

As he asks me to marry him, he opens the gift box for me to see. Nestled on a blue velvet cushion is a beautiful princess cut diamond ring. I know nothing about diamonds, but even I can see that this is a good clarity and a good cut. Like better than good in fact. The band is white gold, and it is the most perfect engagement ring I have ever seen.

"Yes," I say, tears filling my eyes. "Of course I'll marry you."

Cullen grins up at me, his face a mixture of joy and relief. I can't believe even a small part of him thought I might say no to being his wife. He's the love of my life and I tell him that often enough.

He slips the ring out of the box and onto my finger and I hold my hand up, smiling at the way it looks on my finger.

"Thank you," I say.

"Do you like it? I won't be offended if you don't. We can exchange it for a different one," he says.

"Cullen, shh," I laugh. "I love it."

"Merry Christmas," he says with a smile. "Now you are mine forever."

I love the sound of that, and I lean in and kiss him.

"I love you," I say. "And I love my ring. It's definitely the best Christmas present ever."

"Oh, well then if that's the case, I'll just return your other presents," Cullen says, smirking at me.

"You might want to rethink that idea," I say. "When you see what I'm going to do to you to say thank you."

I get up and drag Cullen up and we run for the stairs. I feel like I'm running toward the first day of the rest of my life, a life I will live side by side with my protector, my lover, my husband, and my soulmate.

The End

Coming Soon... Sample Chapters

THE BRIDE'S BROTHER

Chapter 1

Evelyn

The high school photos had to be my favorite so far. As I went through the scenes of the couple sitting on the seats where they'd met, by their lockers and where he'd first asked her on a date to the cafeteria, my heart fluttered a little. It was a lovely story, but the way I'd captured every scene in different lighting made me feel very happy. In these pictures, I had told their history, the cracks on the wall, the rust on bars, the chipped paint, broken ceiling corners, and the beaming smiles of the couple themselves. It was fairy-tale-like and yet it was real.

I was so in love with what I had created.

There was one problem, though. Given that they were my cousin's friends, and they were both blue-collar workers, I hadn't been able to charge them what I normally would. Not that it was much, but even then, they had trouble paying for my photography.

I looked at the time once again, wondering just how long I'd been in the cafe. I didn't think they had a limit of how long you could stay after buying the cheapest possible drink, which was an iced Americano, but I was ready to pack my things and leave the second any of the staff started heading towards me.

I needed to charge more, and I needed more high-profile clients so I could have something left over after paying my exorbitant, blood-sucking New York rent to repair my broken AC. My inability to call a repairman until I got my next paycheck was once again a wakeup call. I continued on with my edits, anxious to complete it as quickly as possible so that I could post some of them on Instagram and attract some potential new clients.

I had no connections nor did I know any socialites, so this was my only way. This was my fault, though. Rather than spend time during college going to parties and meeting people, I was taking on as many part-time jobs as I could and ignoring the social aspect, which I now realize was the most important aspect of my job.

Sighing, I continued on with my work. When I briefly glanced up to look around the cafe, I met the eyes of someone standing in a corner. She seemed to have purchased some pastries and was sipping on her coffee. However, her attention on me was rapt. It immediately made me self-conscious because this was also sure to draw the attention of the cafe staff.

Annoyed, I looked away from her and continued with my work, but I sent a deep frown her way, hoping that this would immediately put her off showing any interest in me.

I returned to my photos and forgot all about her until I felt someone start to pull out the stool beside me. It was to be expected since I had opted for the window seats rather than an actual table in order to curry more grace for over-staying, so I wasn't bothered, but when I noticed that the person seemed to have their entire focus on me, I looked up and was shocked to see it was the girl that was staring at me before.

She was stunning in a way that made me unable to look away, even though I was unhappy at her intrusion. Her hair was bone straight, shiny, sleek, and jet black, and her eyes were the most beautiful shade of green I had ever seen. Due to my annoyance earlier, I hadn't noticed any of these, but now as I stared straight at her, I couldn't help noticing her beauty.

"Hello?" She smiled.

I nodded in response. "Hi."

"I'm sorry I was a bit nervous to come over." Her glance went to my laptop. "I see you're working, so I know I'm interrupting you." She smiled apologetically, but continued to stare at me. "Sorry," she said. "I've loved your work for so long; I just can't believe I'm actually meeting you in person. You do gorgeous work and I'm just so happy to meet you."

Upon hearing this, all of my annoyance, doubts, and reservations immediately dissipated because she was obvi-ously someone who followed me on social media and loved my work, so how could I in any way be offended or put off by her approach?

Instantly, I gave her a heartfelt smile and offered my hand for a handshake.

I'm sorry," I apologized. "I'm just a bit stressed, so I came off unapproachable. Thank you for coming over regardless. I'm so glad to know you know and like my work; that means so much to me. I mean, I just started so I don't have that many followers."

"You just need time for the right kind of people to find you," she said earnestly. "Because your work is unique... very rustic and special. Most people just go anything pink and glittery."

I nearly laughed out loud at this, liking her even more because she was a hundred percent right. "Thank you so much for saying that; your words mean the world to me because I was just thinking how my style might be affecting my ability to eat." I laughed. "And that maybe, I should start going the way that everybody else is going."

"Oh no!" she exclaimed, nearly startling me. "Don't. You're unique. Please don't change."

I shrugged and laughed. "It's very kind of you to say that, but New York charges even for air, so I might have to start following the crowd soon."

She looked suddenly bright and happy. "You know what, I want to work with you. The style I want is exactly right up your alley. Everyone else in my family didn't seem too taken with it. I'm pregnant and just so exhausted, so I didn't push too hard. But now that I've run into you against all odds, I think it's a sign from the universe."

I stared at her, my mouth nearly open, wondering for a moment if she was playing a trick on me.

"Are you serious?" I asked.

She nodded happily. "I am. We already have a wedding planner and all that, and she's been suggesting photographers to me, but I haven't paid any attention because I hated all her big name photographers. And... I just know you'll love the location. It's a small ancient church. Its stained-glass windows are the most beautiful things you'll ever see, and its domed ceilings are painted with angels."

My mouth nearly fell open. "Are you joking? Where is this?"

"In the Hamptons," she replied.

I thanked my lucky stars that I wouldn't have to travel too far, but still, all of this was sounding too good to be true. I decided to have a little faith, especially since I didn't have much of a choice.

"Sounds wonderful," I replied.

"So you'll do it?" she asked breathlessly

"Of course. I'm just wrapping up the project I was working on, so I'm free and would love to photograph your wedding."

"Wow, this really seems like fate. I'm so excited."

"Me too," I agreed, more relieved than she could imagine.

"There is the small matter of how quickly you can wrap up. Due to my pregnancy it has to be next week, but no biggie, ha ha," she laughed. "So can you start next week."

I nodded. "Okay."

"Great. I want all the little moments captured."

I nodded enthusiastically.

"I'll be picking out a dress next week. Can you be there so you can take photos of the event and you also can meet the wedding planner and anyone else necessary. I haven't really thought about a dress preference, but if I eventually see one that I fall in love with, I want the moment captured."

I completely understood all that she was saying. I was so excited at the concept that I wanted to kiss her.

"I know what you want, and it's just the challenge I need. I'll make it special for you, trust me."

She released a deep sigh of relief, then she rose to her feet.

"I'm so happy right now. You have no idea. Alright, let me get back and make the preparations;

I'll reach out to you next week?"

"Alright," I said and immediately began to fumble through my laptop bag for a business card, but she stopped me with a gentle hand on my arm.

"No need," she said.

"I follow you, remember? Your details are on Instagram, and I can always direct message you."

"You're right," I said, a bit sad that she wasn't giving me her number. I wanted hers in case she forgot about me or changed her mind. I didn't want to sound desperate, but I really needed this follow-up gig.

"Can I have your number now either way?" I asked. "If it isn't any trouble. I won't bug you with any messages, but I'll save your name and look forward to your call."

"Of course." She pulled out her phone, and we exchanged numbers.

"Thank you so much," I said, and truly I wanted to hug her, but I found a way to hold myself back.

"No, thank you for being here," she said, and this made me laugh louder than I should have. It drew some attention, perhaps even that of the staff as well, but I didn't care anymore. I had a new client, and once again, all was well with the world. I would survive the month to come, and it was much more than I could ask for.

I watched her leave, and then with more enthusiasm than before, I continued with my work, and in no time, I was done and out of there. Since I no longer had to worry about money, my mind was free to do my best work, but as usual, that anxiousness that this was too good to be true kept me on edge.

Chapter 2

Drake

"Sir?" my secretary called.

What is it?" I asked, trying to keep my voice neutral. It had been a difficult day, starting with a very disappointing and heartbreaking trip to the hospital.

I felt as if I'd been running for so long, and I had come very far. I was used to this pace and I didn't want to slow down, but circumstances I couldn't control were forcing me to.

I was used to putting out fires and finding solutions. It came with running a billion-dollar conglomerate, but this was different. I could never find a solution even if I went to the ends of the earth, and so far, I already had, but I was not giving up. I was going to carry on trying even if all that remained was a dead end.

"Your sister's here to see you, Sir," my secretary replied, and this brightened me up somewhat. She was always a sight for sore eyes, especially now.

"Let her in," I said, happy for the reprieve.

She nodded and left. The door was pushed open and my smiling baby sister walked in.

"Hey," I said.

"I just ran into my favorite photographer," she said, dropping into the seat in front of me.

I nodded warily. "And you want him to replace the photographers that Victoria has recommended?"

She cocked her head. "Not him. Her," she corrected, then frowned. "But to be honest. I don't understand why you're so involved in my wedding plans." But even as the words left her tongue, she felt remorse, and her gaze dropped to the floor.

"I mean... I didn't mean it that way," she said in a low, contrite tone.

"So, how did you mean it?" I asked gently.

"You've never ever involved yourself in little things like this, and you've never stopped me from doing any of the things I truly wanted. So, I don't know why you're so involved in the organizing of my wedding. What difference does it make to you?"

I wished I could tell her the truth. I wished I didn't have to be the bad guy ruining her most important day, but I couldn't tell her. I'd made a promise. One day she would understand why I had to be this way.

"I told you," I said calmly, opening the document on my desk. "You're the one who chose to get married to someone outside our circle, so the society wedding is needed for his sake. What greater chance is there to improve his standing and associate him with us. It's all for your benefit ultimately."

"Drake," she called softly. "I'm serious about this. I was ready to give in and allow you and Mom to have your way, but after seeing her today, it seems like I've been given a second chance. I don't want a big glitzy wedding; I want it in a small, intimate, gorgeous setting, with a few friends and my immediate family."

I ran out of patience.

"No," I said, and got ready to shut her out and go back to work.

"No? Just no?"

I didn't reply to her anymore.

"What if we just elope?" she asked angrily. "Since you're refusing to listen to me, that's an idea. We don't need a wedding anyway."

"Is the venue that important?" I asked, irritated.

"That's what I'm asking you! If it's not so important, then why don't you just let it be?"

"Because we have contacts and people that we need to take the opportunity to honor, and people need to know that we are ashamed of the choice you have made. That we welcome him into our fold and from that forth they must afford him the same respect they give us."

"You talk as though he runs a street cart," she replied bitterly. "He is a lawyer; he meets plenty of high-profile clients every single day, thank you very much."

"He is a first-year associate," I countered. "He needs another ten years to build his relevance in society."

I looked away because it was clear to both of us now that this conversation was over.

She rose to her feet, snatched her purse off the table and exited the office with an angry expression.

I tried not to be affected by her justified anger, because I knew if she was aware of the true reason why I wanted her to have this ridiculously huge wedding, she would not only understand but embrace it with both arms.

For now, all I could do was hope she would be agreeable and cooperate so that this time could pass as smoothly and peacefully as possible.

Liked what you read?
Pre-order the book here:
The Bride's Brother

About the Author

Thank you so much for reading!
If you have enjoyed the book and would like to leave a
precious review for me, please kindly do so here:

Enemy Boss

Please click on the link below to receive info about my latest
releases and giveaways.
NEVER MISS A THING

Or
come say 'hello' here:

Also by Iona Rose

Nanny Wanted

CEO's Secret Baby

New Boss, Old Enemy

Craving The CEO

Forbidden Touch

Crushing On My Doctor

Reckless Entanglement

Untangle My Heart

Tangled With The CEO

Tempted By The CEO

CEO's Assistant

Trouble With The CEO

It's Only Temporary

Charming The Enemy

Keeping Secrets

On His Terms

CEO Grump

Surprise CEO

The Fire Between Us

The Forgotten Pact

Taming The CEO Beast

Hot Professor

Flirting With The CEO

Surprise Proposal

Propositioning The Boss

Dream Crusher

Until He Confesses

Insufferable Boss

Strictly Business

Confessing To The CEO